I0637856

The
Family Album

The Family Album

a novel

kerry kelly

DUNDURN
TORONTO

Copyright © Kerry Kelly, 2012

All rights reserved. No part of this publication may be reproduced, stored in a retrieval system, or transmitted in any form or by any means, electronic, mechanical, photocopying, recording, or otherwise (except for brief passages for purposes of review) without the prior permission of Dundurn Press. Permission to photocopy should be requested from Access Copyright.

Editor: Allister Thompson
Design: Courtney Horner
Printer: Webcom

Library and Archives Canada Cataloguing in Publication

Kelly, Kerry, 1975-
    Family album / Kerry Kelly.

Issued also in electronic formats.
ISBN 978-1-4597-0159-5

    I. Title.

PS8621.E4416F36 2012   C813'.6   C2011-906009-4

1   2   3   4   5   16   15   14   13   12

 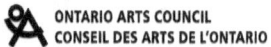

We acknowledge the support of the **Canada Council for the Arts** and the **Ontario Arts Council** for our publishing program. We also acknowledge the financial support of the **Government of Canada** through the **Canada Book Fund** and **Livres Canada Books,** and the **Government of Ontario** through the **Ontario Book Publishing Tax Credit** and the **Ontario Media Development Corporation**.

Care has been taken to trace the ownership of copyright material used in this book. The author and the publisher welcome any information enabling them to rectify any references or credits in subsequent editions.

J. Kirk Howard, President

Printed and bound in Canada.
www.dundurn.com

Dundurn
3 Church Street, Suite 500
Toronto, Ontario, Canada
M5E 1M2

Gazelle Book Services Limited
White Cross Mills
High Town, Lancaster, England
LA1 4XS

Dundurn
2250 Military Road
Tonawanda, NY
U.S.A. 14150

For my parents

1

S HE HATED DONUTS. SHE FELT BAD ABOUT IT, AND VAGUELY unpatriotic, but there it was. She hated the heavy sweetness and the grease stains they left on her napkin and, inevitably, her pants and shirt cuffs. Still, she had been sucking them back wholesale for the past three weeks. Every morning from nine to noon as she made her slow, circuitous march around her office building, solidarity slogans emblazoned across her chest, she did it with a cruller in hand.

She ate them out of boredom, and because she was angry and depressed watching her colleagues staring into their reflections in the mirrored windows of their employer, cursing all those still inside. Really, she ate them because they were the offerings of the dwindling percentage of the public not yet openly hostile about how this little media set-to she found herself embroiled in was cocking up their prime time viewing and access to the news of the day. But she could see that even these rank-and-file supporters of public broadcasting were reaching their tolerance limit. The large, square boxes of full-sized chocolate glazed and plain old-fashioneds had been downgraded to toolbox-shaped containers of sourdough globs and the gross coconut and raisin monstrosities that even children don't like.

The night before, she had even started dreaming about them, waking from a nightmare in which she found herself buried to the chin in a child's bouncy ball castle overflowing with sticky pellets, trying to keep her head from going under as her mother called out to her that she shouldn't get her picket sign dirty. That was just too much. When the alarm went off, she knew she couldn't face another morning pastry and called in sick from not working.

She coughed disdainfully in response to her strike captain's admonishments that she had a responsibility to be there and his persistent reminder that the enemy, who only a few short weeks ago he'd been more than happy to go out with for after-work drinks, were devious, money-grubbing jackoffs and that *they* would not be calling in sick today. "Those sons of bitches will be all over the air talking about how hard they are working to get us back in there ... like they weren't the ones to lock us out. Sonsabitches."

She stared at the stucco ceiling, thinking again what an insidious invention stucco was, how easy it had been to put it up there and how impossible to get it off, and how dated and crappy it looked, while the drone in her ear talked of her duty to make sure the public understood this wasn't their doing.

"We've got nothing to be embarrassed about here, Cyn; we're the ones getting screwed."

She wasn't embarrassed. For the better part of her radio career, Cynthia had found herself having to justify her publicly funded salary to some private-sector rube or another. She had been on the picket line before and had to face the angry comments and valid questions of those who felt they were being used as pawns in somebody else's war. This wasn't her first barbeque. She wasn't embarrassed at all. She was just tired — tired and bloated. She was forty-five and a single mom and slightly arthritic in her left hand and fifteen pounds overweight, and she just didn't damn well feel like going downtown today to march around a building to beg for the chance to do her job.

"I'm really not feeling well, John," she sniffled unconvincingly. "Stop giving me hell and show a little solidarity with this injured comrade, would you."

"I expect to see you here tomorrow, Cynthia, no kidding. People want to see the public faces out here on the block too. No one gives a damn about the electricians. We have got to pressure these bastards into fixing this mess."

She considered reminding him that they worked in radio and no one knew what the hell she looked like anyway. She also toyed with the idea of reminding him that once they fixed this mess, he was going to have to have to work with those "bastards" once again. In the end she just said she'd see how she was feeling tomorrow, hung up, and dropped happily back into bed.

But now that she was free to lie there for the remainder of the day, of course she couldn't. She was all of a sudden antsy and unsure of what to do with this stolen time. The kids had headed off to school and Ellen would already be en route for their walkabout, unaware that Cynthia had pulled 'chute.

Getting out of bed, she headed towards the stairs, resisting the urge to pop her head into the kids' rooms and bear witness to the ungodly chaos they had unleashed. That would only end with Cynthia up to the knees in her son's dirty laundry and on the losing side of a guaranteed fight about "privacy" when her daughter got home, so she pressed on, stopping briefly to notice the carpet on the stairs was decidedly worn and wondering tiredly when the hell the whole house had begun to fall apart. In the kitchen she started a pot of coffee, and her mood, which had lately taken to turning on a dime, improved exponentially. She took immense pleasure in the scent of the beans as she ground them, the splash of cold distilled water hitting the glass carafe, and the feel of the warm ceramic of her favourite mug in her hands.

Taking that first sip of the first decent cup of coffee she'd had since this whole pain in the ass started, Cynthia Wilkes sat at her kitchen table, kicked up her feet, and allowed herself to consider that perhaps her life was not an entire disaster. She still had two kids home with her, and all three bright and healthy. She was fairly confident that they were happy, if sometimes unbearable in the way that only adolescents can be. She owned her own home, quite the feat if you considered the city she lived in and the work she did. Plus, she noted as the warmth from her cup slowly began to soothe her stiff fingers, a few achy joints aside, she was holding up pretty well. In fact, only just the other day a man had called her stone cold fox. Well, to be precise, the term he'd used was stone cold silver fox, and the man was the homeless and most certainly alcoholic fellow who guarded, of his own volition and seemingly with no financial motivation, the door to her neighbourhood public library. Still, he'd sounded sincere.

She also knew, from unfortunately not-uncommon experience, that this pissing contest at work would eventually come to an end, and while she would probably end up going back to a place that was just a little bit worse than before, she would be going back, which wasn't a guarantee for everyone walking around down there.

For Cynthia, things would generally continue to roll along as they had for the past decade or so. While the past held its traumatic moments, and whose had not, hers had been a voyage of generally placid seas, one on which she was afforded all necessities and more than a few perks. It was without question more than most had. This thought didn't make her feel much better, which she found mildly surprising and a bit pretentious. It was a little too "First World problems" for her liking, and she didn't really want to think about it, so she decided that not thinking would be the order of the day. She brought the mug up close to her face to inhale the warmth and aroma and turned her head to stare idly out the picture window at the fading remnants of her summer garden.

From this position she did not see the girl standing on the front porch, staring at her intently. The girl was ten years old. She seemed younger, unless you looked into her eyes. Her name was Abigail and she was standing fascinated, on tiptoe, watching Cynthia sipping on her morning coffee with her slippered feet up on the opposite chair.

Abigail knew Cynthia. She knew *of* her. They were strangers really, though they had much in common. Most valuable among them, in Abigail's mind, was the family name she saw engraved on the antique mailbox beside the door. This was how she knew she had arrived at the right house. Her hand had already started to lift up the lid when she spotted Cynthia walking across the kitchen, and she froze. She had been standing there like a statue ever since, only her eyes moving as she surveyed all she could through the window.

Abigail had come to the house by herself, unannounced, not expecting anyone to be home. She had hoped only to leave a polite note, thoughtfully composed in her best cursive writing. Abigail had the best penmanship in her class by far, though this hadn't garnered the recognition she felt it should. But Cynthia … Mrs., Ms.? Wilkes was there. So Abigail was stuck. She wondered whether Cynthia would hear if she dropped the mailbox lid, and even if she didn't, would Abigail's footsteps on old wooden porch slats give her away? She knew she should not be there and was now a little frightened and unsure about what to do next. She also felt exhilarated and did not want to waste a golden opportunity to observe this woman up close, only ever having been able to look at her from the back window of her parents' car.

The woman had grown to be an almost mythic legend in young Abigail's mind, a person who was hardly mentioned and never discussed without an awkward, careful tone creeping into all voices. Cynthia Wilkes was a secret that Abigail had uncovered one day when she stumbled across the old photos her father kept out of sight of her mother in faded cloth-covered albums stored on the bottom shelves of his office bookcase. She was a voice Abigail would listen to from time to time, her ear buds jammed in tightly, the volume almost inaudibly low and the thrill of doing something dangerous and covert running through her body, even though she was unsure of why it should be so.

Abigail waited another minute, watching Cynthia stare out the window, before her arm began to protest. Then, murmuring something that might have been *"Carpe diem,"* which she'd heard in a movie once and been suitably impressed, she dropped the lid with a thud and began knocking sharply on the door.

Cynthia jumped, sloshing coffee onto the table, first startled, then annoyed at being disturbed so early in the day, as well as by a latent Catholic guilt that equated staying home to some kind of sin. Through the glass she saw a little girl in a bright red rain slicker and matching hat and noted that it wasn't raining. But she was still too tired and dazed by all the not thinking she'd been doing to look much closer. She opened the door with the assumption that today she'd be trading a breakfast of donuts for that of Girl Guide mint chocolate wafers.

So it came as quite a shock to find that she was staring at her daughter. To be more precise, she was looking at the wide blue eyes, pointed chin, and dark Irish curls of her daughter. But it was not Julia. She was already at school and was not a ten-year old Girl Guide but an angst-ridden seventeen-year-old. As the little girl shyly smiled Julia's smile, a sight Cynthia didn't see nearly often enough and very much missed, the cogs in her brain creaked into action and she recognized this child as her daughter's sister, her ex-husband's child. Abigail Wilkes. The little bundle whose unexpected arrival had led to the hasty dissolution of what had, up to that point been, for both parties, a pretty satisfying marriage.

Cynthia suddenly felt very much older than forty-five, and her arthritic hand ached as she reached to slam the door shut before another synapse fired and she remembered herself to be the kind of woman who didn't slam the door in faces of smiling young girls in red rain slickers.

Abigail's eyes grew wide and she remained silent as Cynthia slowly swayed in the doorway, her mouth hanging open and her hand still on the door. Cynthia craned her neck left and right, looking for traces of Tom and his new wife — not so new now, Cynthia supposed, but it was how she had thought of Jennifer ever since Tom had decided to make their little affair legit and married her. After that it seemed inappropriate to call her children's stepmother "That Whore." If ever they decided to make an impromptu visit, they would of course choose to do so when Cynthia was wearing a bathrobe and playing hooky from the picket line, but it seemed the little girl was alone.

Cynthia heard the girl swallow nervously before abruptly sticking out her hand and almost shouting: "I am Abigail Wilkes. How do you do? You have a lovely home. May I come in?"

Smiling in spite of herself at the voluminous introduction, Cynthia couldn't think of anything else to do but and accept the tiny hand, shaking it gently up and down.

"And I am Cynthia Wilkes. I know who you are...." Then, making the most logical assumption at the reason for this unlikely morning guest, she added, "Are you here to see Julia or Ben? They've gone to school."

Abigail shook her head. She wasn't here to see her siblings. She was standing on her father's first wife's front porch because she wanted to be a writer. Along with taking the prize for penmanship, she was the best storyteller in her class, and she thought she'd be a really great writer too. Her brothers and sister were good at it. People told them so all the time — even Ben, who didn't care about anything but sports. "They're naturals, it's in the genes," she'd heard her father say, though never when her mother was around.

But was not in Abigail's genes. She didn't think she could have inherited a lick of talent for it from either of her parents, one a boring lawyer the other an even more boring administrative assistant. No, what came naturally to Matthew, Julia, and Ben came from Cynthia, and Abigail hadn't gotten any of it. And it wasn't fair, because writing was what Abigail wanted to do more than anything else in the whole wide world. Way more than she wanted to be in those stupid dance classes her mother was always signing her up for.

So she had decided that if she hadn't been born with the writer's touch, she'd earn it — in fact, she'd learn it. And she couldn't think of anybody better to teach her than Cynthia, who told stories all the time on the radio, whose name Abigail had seen in real magazines, who had even written a book, a copy of which sat amongst the collection of worn and highly abused books that lined the walls of Matthew's recently vacated bedroom. Abigail was hanging all her ten-year-old hopes that Cynthia would be able to offer her the tools she'd need to spin some stories of her own. Ones that were good enough to make people want to read them. And she told her so.

Cynthia took this all in with arms crossed, leaning against the frame for support. She examined the child carefully, looking for hints of mockery or mental health concerns around the edges of the request, but couldn't find any. The girl looked so sincere, and so much like Julia, like Tom, that she couldn't stop staring. There had been a short time, still vivid in Cynthia's mind, when she had hated this little person more than anybody on earth, with the exception of the girl's mother. Hated her very existence and what it meant for her and for her little girl and her sons, all so young at the time. It seemed ridiculous now, shameful that she could have ever felt this way about a child. Abigail was only a child, a sweet little thing too, it seemed, so guileless, earnest, and hopeful. Just a little girl. Then Cynthia's parenting instincts suddenly kicked in, and she looked up and down the street again for a sign of either of Abigail's talentless parents.

"How did you get here?"

"I took a cab."

"Your parents put you in a cab ... alone? To *my* house?"

Cynthia was incredulous until she thought a little bit about Tom, something she almost never did any more, and suddenly didn't completely rule it out. She shook her head, trying to coax her brain into keeping up with the conversation she was, still unbelievably, having. It felt like trying to get directions in a foreign language.

"Oh, no. They think I am at school. My mom wouldn't ever let me come here on account of the way you think you are soooo much better than everybody else," Abigail said, stretching out the syllables in imitation before she paused at the sight of Cynthia's raised eyebrows and blushed deeply. "Oh. No offence," she said, charging ahead. "I googled your address and came by myself."

Cynthia found that she was smiling through the insult, at this odd little kid and the outrageous request. Coming back to herself, she also remembered how young the girl was.

"So no grown-ups know where you are right now?"

"You do," Abby countered. She was Tom's daughter all right.

"Yes. Fair enough. I'll rephrase ... you are telling me you snuck out of school to come here, even though you think your mother will disapprove?"

"For sure she will.

"Don't you think that's a little dangerous? That you might get into some trouble doing things like that?"

"I know that people need to suffer for their art."

"I've heard that."

"Writing made Dorothy Parker suicidal."

"Oh."

"I love Dorothy Parker."

"Huh. And you're ..." Cynthia quickly did the actual math and was reminded of the longevity of certain kinds of aching, "... ten years old?"

"Yes, but I'm a very advanced reader. The best reader in my class."

"I would imagine."

"I'm the best storyteller too. My teacher said." As proof, Abigail pulled two hard-covered black notebooks out of the backpack at her feet. "Would you like to see some of my work?" Holding out the books, she said offhandedly, "These notebooks are the same ones that Hemingway used.... Well, not these exact ones, I bought these new. But he liked this style."

"You're a Hemingway fan as well?" Cynthia said, taking the books and trying not to sound like an asshole grown-up.

"Yeah, he's okay, I guess. Not so funny."

"I can see that." Then, tucking the books under her arm, "Okay, so I think it would probably be an excellent idea if we let your parents know that you are here."

Abigail's pale, lightly freckled face went a shade whiter as she started to visualize the potential consequences of being found out of school, on her own, and in the company of this particular person.

"Yeah, I guess. It'd probably be better if you called my dad."

Better for who? thought Cynthia, although she had to admit if you were going to have to pick the lesser of two evils here, you'd have to pick Tom.

"Good idea."

Afraid that she may never again have this kind of opportunity, Abigail asked, "Can I come inside while you call? Maybe you can read some of my stuff while we wait?"

This had not been part of Abigail's initial plan, but now that she was here, she found herself desperate to see inside the house where her siblings lived, having already taken in all that she could see around Cynthia through the open door.

Ignoring a sudden longing for the simple drama of the picket line, and even for the donuts, Cynthia stepped from the doorway back into the house. "Come on in then."

Abigail didn't wait to be asked twice, hopping into the foyer, dropping her bag at the same time. She scanned the living room, taking in all the exotic accoutrement of her siblings' primary dwelling.

"That's Julia's," she said, pointing at a raggedy pink sweatshirt tossed over a wing chair by the fireplace, a favourite reading spot when she was willing to share common space with the other members of the household. "I have one too. Matthew got me one when he went away to school. Mine doesn't fit any more, though."

"Oh. That's too bad." But the wistfulness in the statement seemed to have already passed as Abigail headed towards the piano at the back of the room, giving the ivories an exuberant pounding, all the while craning her neck see what else was to be seen in the dining room. "Cool piano!"

"That it is ... though maybe it's a bit early to be quite so ... musical." Cynthia was mesmerized by how at home this little stranger seemed in her house. Not so much because of the liberties she was taking, well that too, though it was the divine right of ten-year-olds to think the world really was designed just for them. It was the way she blended into the room, so much like Julia and like Matthew, eyes on everything her hands hadn't gotten a hold of yet, the constant commentary and unnerving energy. Ben was the only child who favoured Cynthia both in looks and temperament. Abigail acted just like one of the kids — but she wasn't, at least not in this house. Sobered, Cynthia put on what the *real* kids called her serious voice.

"Okay then, why don't we get you a drink or something while I call your dad."

Abigail turned two saucer eyes towards Cynthia and put to shame the display of sorrow felt over an outgrown sweatshirt. "I guess."

"Maybe I can wrangle up a Pop Tart to sweeten the deal?"

"Really? I've never tried one before. My mom won't let me have them. She says they are evil. Oh … sorry."

"Well … I'm not your mom," Cynthia replied sweetly as she reached for the box, and taking some satisfaction in it.

Once Abigail was set up at the kitchen table, well-occupied by her snooping, Cynthia took extra care in her preparation of this mid-morning snack as she gathered her thoughts about the impending call.

It wasn't like they didn't talk. She and Tom spoke often enough, but no more than was necessary to ensure the basic survival of their shared dependents. They never chatted. They didn't share or empathize or entertain. While theirs had been recognized by their acquaintances as a remarkably civil divorce considering the circumstances, it had never been a comfortable one. From the beginning Tom had been too ashamed and overwhelmed to offer any explanation or apology, and Cynthia far too humiliated to ever let him try. So, with the exception of one no-holds-barred throwdown fight that neither of them had ever mentioned again, they had opted for a crude but effective emotional amputation that had allowed them to move swiftly from intimate life partners to functional associates in the care and preservation of their children.

Even before she dialed the number, Cynthia could picture him when he picked up the phone. She could still imagine him at his desk, shirtsleeves rolled up, one hand reaching aimlessly for the freshest cup of coffee, the other being subjected to an oral assault as he systematically bit each nail down to the quick. It had been more than a decade since she'd seen him like that, but she was sure the scene hadn't changed. She knew that people can become strangers to you overnight, but the little things that make up a person, those habits and peccadilloes, they don't change.

The toaster popped, filling the air with scent of fruit and plastic, synonymous with her children's particular breakfast poison, and Cynthia was yet again jolted back to the situation at hand. She served up a plate of piping hot treats, having stuck one in every slot of her six-slice toaster, and was pleased to see the look of expectation on Abigail's face.

"Don't just go diving in there," she cautioned, seeing Abigail reaching out. "Count to a hundred or you'll burn yourself." It was one thing to offer forbidden treats to your ex-husband's child, another entirely to maim her. Abigail's eyes had finally found a fixed focal point as she rapidly mouthed her countdown, and Cynthia picked up the phone, punching in a number she rarely used but still knew off by heart.

"Thomas Wilkes's office," an aging, smoke-damaged voice responded. It had not escaped Cynthia's attention that once the news of Tom's affair had gone public and Jennifer had left the firm to avoid the gossip and the judging eyes, Tom's next choice of office assistant had been a middle-aged, homely, and married chain-smoker. It was the first time Cynthia had to grudgingly admit that perhaps Mrs. Wilkes the second wasn't as dumb as she looked.

"Hello, Margery, it's Cynthia Wilkes calling for Tom."

"Oh." These calls always seemed to begin with an "oh." "Oh yes, I will pass you through."

"Hi. Everyone okay?" Calling at work usually meant at least a code orange family emergency; suspension, broken limb, the visual presence of at least one bodily fluid.

"Hi. Yes. Well, I think so."

"Good. So no hospitals, prisons, missing children alerts?"

"Well, not missing so much as misplaced," Cynthia offered.

"Sorry? I'm not following you. Is everyone okay?" Tom repeated, genuine concern now entering his voice. She knew she was being a bit cryptic, but she was never her best when she was talking on the phone with Tom. Their calls were always rapid and perfunctory, and she never had enough time to recall how they used to talk to one another. She was better at it in person.

"Everyone is safe, but ..." she stalled, trying to figure out what to say, aware of how still the gadabout little girl had become, of how intently she was listening.

"What's wrong Cyn, spit it out." He was so impatient, she couldn't help thinking, always in a rush to get to the point.

"I am. I am trying to say that your daughter is here."

"And what? Wait, I thought you said she was at school. Was she lipping off to the history teacher again?"

"No, not that daughter. What I mean is ... what I'm trying to tell you is that *your* daughter is here. Abigail."

"What?"

"Abigail is here. She is fine. She's having a snack right now. She got here about twenty minutes ago. I thought you should know."

"What the hell is she doing at your house?" The tone was still short, but confusion was the key undertone now.

"Well, I am not entirely sure. It's not like I was expecting her," Cynthia replied, trying to sound cheerful and smiling slightly at Abigail, wishing she had made the call in the other room so that she didn't have to temper her annoyance for the sake of the girl.

"How did she get there? She's supposed to be at school."

"Yes, she mentioned that. It's my understanding that she took a taxi."

"Are you telling me that they let a ten-year-old get in a cab?" His voice was rising.

"Well, I'm no star witness here, Counsellor Tom, but I am under the impression that the school is currently unaware of her whereabouts as well."

"Oh my god. Okay. Well, what do we do about this?"

"I am not sure what your plan should be. Again, may I remind you that I didn't orchestrate this little get-together." Then, looking over at the dark curls hung low over the plate, the treats untouched and getting cold, "As pleasant a surprise as it may have been. Perhaps you could come and pick her up, Tom."

"Right sorry. Oh so ... right. That's probably ... sorry." Presumably not knowing what to say next, Tom said nothing, silence burning up the line between them for an interminable few seconds. She could see him now, a hand running roughly through his hair as he tried to come to a plan of action ... something he was infuriatingly bad at. Tom had built a life on the uninspiring combination of reaction and inaction.

"Ah, Cyn. I don't know what's going on, but I'm really sorry about this. I know it must be awkward for you."

The sound of her name from that voice, tinged with sympathy, a reminder to both of them that she had been the loser in what had transpired, that tone of victim empathy, it was not something she was willing to tolerate on this particular morning.

"Just get over here, would you Tom?" she ordered sharply before hanging up.

"I guess he's pretty mad," Abigail said from underneath her sheath of hair.

"Maybe a little. He's on his way to get you."

It was evident to both of them that neither was looking forward to this. Dropping into a chair at the table, Cynthia pulled the plate into the middle and grabbed a tart. Breaking it in half, she passed a piece to Abigail, who accepted, her face unreadable as she nibbled on a corner, though the thrill seemed lost. They sat in silence for a while as Cynthia tried to process some of what had happened in the short time since she'd opened her eyes only an hour before. Looking over at the glum little face taking her in from the corner of those big blue eyes, Cynthia decided she might as well try to cheer her up a little, because she was probably in for a rough ride when she got home.

"So you were saying you're a Dorothy Parker fan?"

"I adore her," Abigail said, some animation returning.

"So how did that … come about?" Cynthia asked, fishing for a way around asking "isn't that a little old for you?" with little success.

"You think I'm too little to like grown-up books?"

"No, no. Just wondering where you might have come across her." She did not add, *Considering your dad can barely stand to read the paper and I'm pretty sure your mother is illiterate.*

"I found it in Matthew's room. You know, his room at our house. I am going to read all the books he left behind. I'm allowed. He said so."

"Ah," said Cynthia, prickling a little at the mention of her son's second home. "Fair enough."

Her eldest son had opted to spend the summer before his final year at his father's place. It was a bigger space closer to his summer job and had its own entrance, which, at twenty, she had been told was an absolute necessity. She had resisted the idea, and Matthew had accused her of bordering on the ridiculous, requesting that she not to get all "mom" about this. But none of his valid reasoning had made it any easier for Cynthia to take, and she had not handled the situation with that much grace … or any, really. She remembered with embarrassment hovering in the doorway as he'd packed up an impressive number of boxes full of those books. Some of them had been hers, and she had said so, removing them from the pile even though she didn't want them, hadn't even thought about them in years.

She could see Matt slowly extricating himself from the routines and traditions of the family since he started away at school, shedding her influence as he tried to figure out who he was going to be and treating her care and advice like some sort of poisoned apple. That hurt her, even though her friend Ellen assured her that it was natural and absolutely necessary to ensuring he could function as an adult. That had been cold comfort, and she'd remained a little petty and distant after he left, leading to a chill between mother and son that hadn't thawed entirely before he left to go back out west.

At the moment, if she were honest she could admit that she was 0 for 2 in relationships with her oldest kids, and with Ben gearing up for a season of hockey with Tom filling the role of ultimate hockey parent, she had been feeling a little usurped of late. It struck her as funny that while her kids were flocking to their father, his daughter was risking a backlash at home and at school for the chance to hang out with her. She looked at the clock only to realize that Tom was at least a half an hour away. Getting up to fill her coffee cup, she spied the Hemingway-approved notebooks she'd been handed earlier. Picking up the first one and selecting another tart from the pile, she nudged the plate back towards Abigail with an encouraging nod and flipped open the book.

"Well, we have some time to kill, kiddo. Let's take a look-see, shall we?"

2

THE ROSES ON THE NIGHTSTAND GENTLY BOBBED THEIR over-bloomed heads, lulled by the steady vibration of Jennifer's foot tapping on the hardwood floor. As angry as she was, it still registered somewhere in the back of her mind that she'd need to be replacing them soon. She could never seem to turn it off, her eye for order, though she found it exhausting.

"So she just hopped in a cab and went over there ... all on her own? This is what you are saying to me?"

"Yes. For the fortieth time, yes. That is what I am saying to you," Tom replied in that infuriatingly patronizing way of his. Lately there had hardly been a conversation where he wasn't either badgering her like a hostile witness or treating her like some sort of dim-witted charity case who'd garnered his sympathy.

She knew the story backwards and forwards, at least as much as he had been willing to share. She'd memorized every fact and minute detail, looking for any change in the timeline, any added snippets of conversation, and for hours now they had all been rolling around in her head like billiard balls on the felt, but she just couldn't sink one. It simply made no sense. Abby going AWOL from school — God knows what could have happened to her — and ending up at his ex-wife's house. And then, after a decade of Cynthia basically ignoring her existence, Abby was invited right on in for breakfast, no problems. Tom racing over to pick her up and then deciding it would be great to catch up over coffee like all of a sudden everyone had just decided to make up, everything forgiven and best of friends? And finally the whole stupefying idea of sending Abby over there again for some sort of bizarre after-school writing workshops? Who the hell suggested that? And why had the other agreed? Jennifer had heard it all, but she could not accept what she'd heard. She could not see past the craziness of it, or her growing anger. By the time three hours had passed, she had settled into a quiet and dangerous kind of furious tempered only by confusion and exhaustion, and the fact that they were going to be late for a dinner party.

Looking at herself in the mirror, Jennifer thought that, if nothing else, she could take comfort in the fact that at least she was dressed the part of the happy wife and expectant guest. Dress for the job you want, her mother had always told her. She was aware of the fact that she was beautiful. She was one of the lucky, vain ones who could truly believe it. The knowledge often gave her strength in difficult or stressful times, probably more often than it should have, but tonight it had no effect on her, and she sat on the edge of the bed in her tastefully expensive dress and an agitated silence punctuated with the occasional questions or declarations of disbelief, because she just could not fathom that this was how her evening had turned out. It was so unlike the way she had foolishly allowed herself to imagine when she'd walked in the door at the end of the day to find Tom and Abby snuggled together in a blanket on the couch, watching one of Ben's idiotic sports-disaster movies and laughing hysterically.

Then she hadn't been the slightest bit upset — even as she took in that Tom was wearing sweatpants and surrounded by a sea of dirty dishes with all of her expensive silk throw pillows tossed amid other random junk scattered from the kitchen to the living room. She had even bitten back her comments at evidence that the perfectly assembled tray of appetizers she had so painstakingly created earlier was going to need a major reno. She loved watching the two of them together and was thrilled to think that Tom had managed to extricate himself from his office duties to spend a little time with his daughter before the adults headed out for the evening.

Tom had been working so much lately. To see him there relaxed at home was worth the mess. In fact, at that moment, if Jennifer was the type of woman to allow herself the luxury of self-reflection, she would have considered herself perfectly content. And it was not a state she often found herself in.

It had been very short-lived, lasting only up until she broke the spell by asking what they were up to, to find they'd been in that same position for hours and that Abby hadn't gone to school that day, or more correctly, that she had decided not to stay there. It was further eroded when she learned of the reason. Her ten-year-old daughter had stolen money from her purse, said goodbye to her mother with a straight face, before walking away from the schoolyard, not telling a soul, and hopping into a car with a strange man to travel to a neighbourhood she knew nothing about — to spend the morning with Cynthia Wilkes, of all people. For someone whose entire life experience up to this point could be the textbook example of the cautionary cliché "expect the worst," Jennifer was surprised that she could still have those rare moments of naive optimism push their way through the weeds of reality, blooming so briefly, delicate and lovely. She always felt so betrayed when she couldn't keep herself from thinking that they might survive.

But the final blow was to learn that this bad, so extremely dangerous and unacceptable behaviour, the lying and the risk, had been practically endorsed by her husband — who hadn't even bothered to call her when he found out about it. Who had since said nothing to their daughter about her actions, except making some vague statement to "follow your heart, but use your head next time" while plying her with attention and crappy food, leaving Jennifer in shock and without any forewarning to play the heavy and send Abby fleeing to her room in tears as she aimed a series of "I hate yous" like tiny daggers straight into Jennifer's heart.

"So she just went there and spent the morning with your ex-wife. And you just think this is all fine and dandy?"

"No, of course not. But what do you want me to do, crucify her? She's ten and she's precocious and she was curious, that's all. She has been asking questions, you know that, and you know it was hard on her having Matthew go back to school this year. It's lonely being an only child, especially one who is too smart for her own good. I think she just wanted to see where the other kids spend their time."

Abby had been asking questions, more and more lately. The other day he had found her rooting through the bottom shelves in his office where he kept some old albums, not hidden exactly, but kept discreetly out of Jennifer's view. He knew that Abigail had flipped through them before from the times that he had done the same, but he had never offered her the chance to do it with him.

In a way Tom knew this whole escapade was his fault. He had up till now neatly avoided any conversations his daughter attempted to broach on the subject of Cynthia and his previous life. Cynthia had been the central piece of that life, his memories for so long — they'd met as kids — but out of respect for Jennifer, he had made almost his entire childhood an off-limits area for the girl. He did it even though he knew she was burning with questions, and that she probably had a right to be. A father's history isn't his alone, no matter how much he'd like to keep it that way, or to try to rewrite or erase it. The truth was, he hadn't been protecting Jennifer as much as Abby or himself. He wanted desperately to keep her unaware, for a little longer, for as long as he could, about the nature of her birth and the foundations of their current family structure, wanting to hold on to the one member of the family who still might consider him a bit of a hero.

But she was too smart and the questions had been getting too precise and more frequent. He should have dealt with it instead of letting her take matters into her own hands. Instead, he let her make the choices. He knew that she had made dangerous ones, and he was just living with the fallout. It was sort of a pattern with him.

"Now she has seen the place, and met their mom, you know that she listens to Cynthia's show, even though she thinks its some kind of crime. She probably thinks Cyn's some kind of celebrity, and kids get a kick out of that. We have never really told her it's okay for her to talk about it, and let's face it, we don't think it is. So now it's done and she is home and safe and no worse off for it except for a tongue-lashing — well-deserved — and a little too much sugar." Abby was being raised on the low-sugar, low-fat, low-preservative, low-taste diet Jennifer enforced to keep herself thin, her daughter healthy, and her aging husband alive long enough to see Abby through college. His other kids complained bitterly.

"I cannot believe that woman feeds her kids that trash. Toaster tarts? Why didn't she just give her arsenic? She probably did." It was a ridiculous thing to say and Jennifer knew it, but there had to be some way that Cynthia was at fault in some of this. The only innocent bystander as far as Jennifer was concerned was herself.

"Well, it's not like Cyn was expecting her, you know. We should just be thankful she was even there to take her in." This he said fully aware of the risk he took in defending the other Wilkes woman.

"Oh, that's right, Saint Cynthia. Mother to the world's children," Jennifer hissed, but the tirade was cut short when another wave of very real panic suddenly swept over her. "She could have been kidnapped or killed or something."

"She wasn't."

"Anything could have happened to her, Tom. Do you not get that? This is not some small town."

"It didn't."

But Tom got it. As calm as he was trying to be for the both of them now, by the time he'd arrived at Cynthia's place, he had been near panic himself thinking of all of the things that could have gone wrong with this seemingly innocent introduction. He was in such a state of impotent rage and euphoric relief that when he saw Abby sitting safe in Cynthia's kitchen, he was filled with an almost irresistible urge to slap her. He couldn't explain it now; he'd only ever experienced it once before years ago, when a five-year-old Matthew, not paying attention to the warnings, had run and slipped off the edge of the dock at the cottage one early spring, scaring them both senseless. The smack had surprised the little boy but hadn't seemed to have held a lasting effect, though after seeing the look on his face, Tom had not believed he could ever hit one of his kids again and be able look them in the eye.

Seeing the look he was giving Abigail, Cynthia had sprung into action and managed, in that seemingly effortless way she possessed, to defuse the situation, physically standing between father and daughter, soothing him as well as Abby, who had started crying when he burst into the kitchen. As Cynthia calmly recounted her understanding of the morning's events, she offered to make them all something hot to drink, guiding Tom firmly to a chair as his adrenaline ebbed and he felt his knees about to give way.

The three sat there for over an hour. Abby spoke shyly to her father, trying to explain why she'd made such an ill-planned and dangerous trip. Cynthia assured them that while the visit had been very unexpected and was certainly not something she would ever advise Abby to try again on her own, that she was impressed with the girl's writing and the girl as well.

Tom took this in, too overwhelmed to do more than sit in a grateful silence, simply nodding and sipping his tea, allowing Cynthia to carry the conversation. This led to a discussion about why she was home that day and what was going on at work. He had been following the work stoppage — anyone archaic enough to still opt to listen to the radio while in the car had to be somewhat aware of it — but he hadn't known how to ask how Cynthia was coping without it coming down to an awkward conversation about money and support payments. She didn't need for anything, she'd have assured him, a fact he was already well aware of.

They also chatted about the other kids, bringing Matt home for the holidays, and Julia's school applications. She asked after his mother and he her parents, who had all retired to the same small town where Tom grew up and Cynthia had spent her summers. They managed, miraculously, not to stumble on any of the unpleasant, taboo, and hot-button topics strewn like mines in their typical conversations. This was especially impressive, as the most volatile of these was embodied in the curly-headed girl sitting between them, sipping on instant hot chocolate and hanging on every word.

As awful as it had started and as awkward as it still managed to be, Tom was sorry when he noticed his cup was empty. It was one of the best conversations he'd had with his ex-wife, with anyone for that matter, in a very long time. There had once been a time in his life when he had been able to talk for hours, until the sun came up. Not proselytize or argue or debate, but actually think and talk and discuss, conversations that filled you up instead of draining you.

It felt as though they had stumbled back onto a familiar rhythm they had once followed so effortlessly. This was the part of the story Tom had not relayed to Jennifer, though he was sure that, even unspoken, it was the part making her so angry. He was feeling calm and serene and curious about the day, and he knew she could sense it and did not understand, and how could he possibly explain it?

"I know how scary this is for you, and how bad it could have been. I do understand it. But nothing bad *did* happen. Aren't you thankful for that? Trust me, after the way you went at her, I don't think Abby will be planning any solo cab rides in the near future." He had meant to lighten the mood, but as so often seemed to be the case these days, he had misread it entirely, and he actually heard the thud as Jennifer sprang up from the bed.

"How I *went* at her? Right. How terrible of me to be a parent. If it was up to you, next time she'll take the car? Oh no, wait, since they are going to be email pals now, I guess she'll be able to just drop her a line whenever she feels like it and ask her to come pick her up!"

This was in reference to what without a doubt had been the worst decision Tom had made that day, he decided. As they were leaving Cynthia's, Abby, so wonderfully, childishly oblivious to adult subtext, and obviously quite thrilled to see how well everyone had gotten along, had decided she'd been wrong to think that there had ever been an issue about getting to know Cynthia. Her initial plan, which even to her had seemed a bit unlikely to ever come to pass, now seemed less unreasonable, so she made the bold move of inquiring when she would be able to come back for her next "lesson."

Tom, who knew this to be an absolute non-option from his wife's perspective, assumed that it would be for Cynthia as well and was shocked to hear her say that it was something Abby would have to check with her parents about, and they could let her know. She'd gone on to say that in the meantime, if Abby ever wanted to send her some writing to take a look at, she'd be happy to do it.

This could have been nothing more that a magnanimous gesture from the non-parent passing the bad news buck, but somehow to Tom it didn't seem that way, and he was touched by the interest Cynthia was showing in his daughter. It seemed more than simply polite to him, and he thought he still knew her well enough to tell. He found himself strangely proud to find a chance to show Abby off, a way of somehow proving that he could make something good on his own, that Abby had been worth it.

As Abby began to explain that she wasn't allowed to use the Internet yet, he heard himself promising to make her an email account just for this educational purpose and agreeing to talk to her mother when they got home about the occasional in-person visit. In spite of, or maybe because of Abby's delight, regret started to rear its head before he'd even put his key in the ignition.

That regret would have been felt even more keenly if he had been standing in the bedroom with his wife that moment. Now, with her arms crossed and the squint in her icy blue eyes, Jennifer cut a surprisingly imposing figure for someone who in her heyday was commonly referred to as a living Barbie doll. But Tom couldn't see her. He just sighed wearily and turned on the shower, hoping to drown her out and steal a little peace. This had been an unexpected day for him too, but with all the harping and multi-generational estrogen pumping, he hadn't really taken any time to deal with it.

From safe within his warm-water cocoon, he was spared the sight of Jennifer storming over to pick up the clock on the nightstand, its big hand pointing to the top of the dial, the little hand on the seven. She set it back down, cursing, and the delicate roses shook again even harder. She bounced around the bedroom, yanking out suit jackets and socks as though these few actions would somehow change the fact that they were now, without a doubt, going to be obscenely late.

Tom also knew they were late. And he knew it was his fault. First forgetting they had plans at all and sending away the after-school sitter, forcing Jennifer to call, apologize, and ask her back. Then the admittedly rather immature handling of the whole thing with Abby, as well as his absolutely immature refusal to get ready until Jennifer was nearly in tears asking him to — not that she hadn't been in tears the whole damn time she was home. He also knew he was going to be paying for this tardiness for the rest of the evening.

Still, after all the useless, stupid bickering since she had walked in the front door, Tom smiled at the thought of her wandering around the bedroom aimlessly checking the seams of her dress and the curl in her hair while she waited for him. The smile widened when he remembered her exasperated look as she pleaded for him to "hurry the hell up." She was not a woman worth fighting with about these kinds of things, because what she lacked in his brand of reasoning, she made up for in lung capacity. So, as usual, he decided to opt out and just luxuriate for a minute under the warm, steady pressure of the water. It felt somehow like a victory. He didn't stay long, though, because it also felt like he was being a real prick.

He emerged from the bathroom and dressed in the sweater she'd laid out for him, wearing the cologne she always bought for him. She was fiddling in her jewellery box trying to act like she hadn't been pacing the entire time. Walking up behind her to grab his suit jacket, he caught her eye in the mirror and came to stand beside her. She was still so very beautiful. And even though he was older, with the grey in his hair less the appetizer than the main course, he thought he was holding his own.

They made a striking couple, if not at that moment a happy-looking one. Currently they resembled some modernist revision of American Gothic; no smiles, stern eyes. He thought that was pretty clever but bit back the thought before it popped out of his mouth. It was not the time for jokes, he remembered; not nearly time for them to be friends again. As they passed Abby's room, Jennifer opened the door a sliver just to say goodnight but received only a snuffled "G'night DAD" in return for her trouble.

At the car, Tom got into the driver's seat, though they were taking her car, and by the end of the night, if history was any indication, it would be obvious that he would be in no condition to drive home. Even though dinner was at her friends' house, a place he'd never been. It was what she expected, and it was the least he could do. He circled around to open her door as she grasped her elegant appetizer, now more of an apology than an offering. The guests would be far too hungry to care about it by the time they arrived. He looked at the assortment, newly arranged on a silver tray, and even through the excessive layers of cling wrap, it was a pretty display.

Tom, now somewhat ashamed of his earlier behaviour, became more so when they pulled onto the highway to find traffic backed up forever. Out of the corner of his eye he watched her yank out her cell phone and construct her apologies, punching them out on the keyboard pad. His fingers mimicked the action, tapping steadily on the steering wheel.

Seconds later the phone rang and Jennifer picked it up, her voice bright and caustic. "I know. I know. Ha ha. Sooo sorry. Had a crazy day with Abby, wait until I

tell you, unbelievable. Yes. I know. I told him we were
going to be late again, how could we not be when he
never steps into the shower until I'm almost apoplectic
with rage about the fact that we are most certainly going
to be late? Ha ha. They're all the same, I know. Okay, we
are on our way. Oh yes, yes sure go ahead and start, we
totally understand. Bye."

Tom saw the disappointment spread across her face, then
the resignation. He knew that she had tried to make this a
nice night for them, a chance for them to get out together.
She tried so hard at everything, too damn hard. He felt bad
for her, and sorry for himself as well. He was hungry and
his eyes searched in the rearview mirror for the tray in the
back seat, knowing it would be mutiny to suggest another
taste, even though the meal was apparently about to begin
without them. He could see the condensation beading on its
surface, the delicate asparagus wilting, smothered by layers
of protective plastic wrap.

Jennifer hung up and said nothing. Tom, angry at being
the butt of her little hen party jokes, filled the silence. "You
bring it on yourself, you know. You've raised the getting
ready stakes to the point where anything less than an
amber alert meltdown on your end makes dressing a pale,
unexciting task stripped of all sexy danger and risk."

He didn't know why he'd said it. Ostensibly he could say
he had wanted to cut the tension, but as soon as it came out
of his mouth, he know he'd just dug his hole a little deeper.

———••0•••———

She didn't even look at him. She couldn't. It was just little
joke, she knew, exactly the kind of idiot line he threw out

when he was feeling guilty or defensive, but she still couldn't believe he'd said it. After all the crap he had put her through that night, jokes were just cruel and insensitive. And he wouldn't stop. She wanted to hit him.

She hated him sometimes. At first that had surprised her, more than that it had terrified her, to realize how much she could despise him. It was a feeling far beyond offence, or distaste, a real, intense, and passionate hate. It made her sad beyond measure to think about it, even though she knew it was a common feeling between spouses. Her friends even laughed about it. "Two sides of the same coin are love and hate," they would say. Or something like that. Something vaguely literary that made them sound clever and always made her feel stupid and inadequate. "We can't imagine why you'd think you two would be above it."

But her friends hadn't started their marriages by breaking up another one. They didn't get their engagement rings because they were asking for two. Their unions weren't based on the fact that another woman had bowed out of the race. And that made a difference. You knew from the beginning that people were capable of doing things they swore they never would. Or that the line between doing what you wanted and making do was paper-thin. Seeing for yourself how the strongest bonds could snap, it made you careful, very careful.

Tonight she also despised her friends, people who had always been there to feed on her misery and the scandals, and who were always willing to share their best gossip about anyone's problems as long as they were out of earshot, but who refused to hold dinner for an hour so you could enjoy it with them.

"Screw it," Jennifer said quietly. "Screw them, and screw you. Just take me home."

"Jen, we are already on the highway, it won't take that long."

"I said, take me home."

"Listen. I'm sorry, okay. I know I've been a bit of an ass tonight."

"Just take me home. Now. Please." With that Jennifer closed her eyes and rested her head against the glass. Tom turned on the radio and looked for the next exit, understanding that her mind was made up.

"Okay."

———

When they pulled up in front of the house, Jennifer told him to wait in the car so he could take the sitter home before she disappeared inside. By the time he'd dropped the girl off, with a full night's pay and a fancy veggie tray by way of apology for the repeated inconveniences, and made it home, the lights were all off downstairs. In no rush to head up, he cobbled together a meal from the fridge and poured himself a good stiff drink. When he finally climbed the stairs, he peeked into Abby's room, knowing he would find the two of them together, Abby, forgiving in sleep, curled up in Jennifer's arms.

They both looked young and fragile like that. He remembered the months when Jennifer was pregnant with Abby. How hellish and heartbreaking it had been at home, but also how he and Jennifer had come together under all of that pressure and judgment and committed to making a home for their child. She had been so scared and told him how much she needed him. And it had felt so good to be needed, to be able to fix something. To be the one who could soothe her in the night, his arms strong around her, her forehead pressed tightly into his chest, breathing in her clean scent.

That scent was how he fell for her in the first place. She smelled of soap, not passion fruit or eucalyptus or roses, just plain old bar soap. It was what had disarmed him against her other womanly charms. The ones a married man knew to watch out for, at least a man not looking to ruin his life: too much leg or breast exposed, long hair, and longer eyelashes. But her scent was so clean and good. Virtuous. He just couldn't get enough of it. And when he'd first been with her and she would come fresh out of the shower, her face bare and glowing and her hair all piled up in a towel exposing that expanse of skin between her shoulder blades and up to the nape of her neck, he was intoxicated. That smell could right the world's wrongs. And it caused a number of them as well.

It had been such a heady time when they were first together. He thought that even then he knew there was no coming back from the infidelity, even if Jennifer hadn't gotten pregnant. She offered him something that Cynthia couldn't ever have. Cynthia was too focused, too confident, and too strong. She could live without him and he'd known that even before she had had to prove it. He had resented her for it. It was never really that she was successful at what she did, no matter what people thought. He had never wanted her to be less. He loved her and was so proud of her for all she was and what she'd done, but somehow in comparison he'd always felt less. Then Jennifer had come along, so beautiful and smart, though she didn't know it, so young and seductive and in love with him. It had made him feel strong and like a real man, if not a good one. He knew the first time he asked her for a drink after work that he had crossed a line, and he knew that to risk all he had with Cynthia was both unthinkable and inevitable, because a man never feels more powerful, more godlike than when actively destroying his own life. He had called it "living." Being with Jennifer had made him feel alive, so he dove in, hoping in his way that it would all work out in the end.

And maybe it had. But when he'd first heard about the baby, he had been devastated. His love for Cynthia was not something that had ever been in question, not even now. He had been bored and felt neglected, and on the surface was a little jealous of the attention she was getting for her work, the time it was demanding of her. His affair, as exciting, lusty, and erotic as it was, was always supposed to come to an end. Even when the fear that his actions would be the undoing of his life with Cynthia and the kids became a reality, he still could not face it. And when Jennifer had told him she wanted to keep the baby, the first thing he had said to her was that he wished she wouldn't.

It was something he regretted the first time he saw Abby's heart beating on a monitor at the hospital, and something he had not been able to forget or forgive himself for since. That moment, his first introduction to his little girl, was also the moment he knew whatever the cost to him, and so heartbreakingly to those around him, he would spend the rest of his life making it up to her. Even at the expense of his marriage, even if it meant hurting his other children, the ones he had welcomed from the beginning.

He'd stood by Jennifer when she was so frightened and so very much alone. And she let him be there for her, let him take control and make the decisions about how they were going to be a family. In doing that, in believing he was capable of making this life for both of them, she have given Tom the chance to become a better man than he'd been before. She *had* made him better, a better man, and he knew it. For that, and for Abby, he was grateful to her. And he did love her and he was sorry that the comfort she needed right now, she didn't want from him.

3

"Hello."

"Hi, it's Julia."

"Hey, Mouse."

"Do not call me Mouse."

"Sorry, hey, Moose."

"Nice. Loser. So … guess what?"

"What?"

"You will NEVER guess who is here right now."

"Who?"

"Like not in a million years!"

"I'm hanging up now."

"No, wait. It's Jennifer."

"Jennifer who?"

"Jennifer Jennifer, Stepmother Jennifer."

"What?"

"She is, like, sitting in the front room. With MOM."

All of a sudden Matthew was listening, though he had no idea what his sister was talking about. "What's Dad doing there?"

"No Dad," said Julia, triumphant now that she had her brother hooked. "Just Jennifer. Abby's not even here."

"What are you talking about, Jules? Why would Abby be there?"

"Oh my god, haven't you heard? It's like insane, Matt … like bizarre-o land insane."

"What's insane?"

"Abby has, like, started coming over here so Mom can teach her to write or something."

"Excuse me?"

"I don't know, so she can just follow in your footsteps and write the great Canadian novel or whatever. It's idol worship gone to extremes. Its ridiculous."

"What?" Julia now had his full attention, something that had probably not been the case since the mid-nineties.

"Matt, that is not EVEN the weird part, okay? So, like, I come home from school and walk in the door and there they are in the living room, like, having tea or whatever. And so I'm like 'hey.' And Jennifer's like 'Hello, Julia,' all nonchalant and everything, and Mom's just looking at me, all smiley and stuff, but, like, not a real smile, and so I'm like 'Ab's in the kitchen?' cuz it's not even her day to be here or whatever and they are both like 'no.' And so now I am thinking 'oh no, what have they got on me'? But they don't say anything else, like, not a word, so I'm like 'okay' and nod like it's totally not weird that they are both just hanging out drinking tea, even though they've never done it before. I'm guessing maybe it's Ben who's in for it and then Mom's like 'The tea's ready in the kitchen' as if we are normally, like, super tea drinkers or something, and I was just like 'I'll pass' and got the hell out of there. So that's, like, totally weird, isn't it?" Julia asked, as it seemed she'd run out of air.

"Yeah. That is pretty weird. "

"I know, right? So Mom's just like 'hey you ruined my life but let's all just hang out together now?' So weird."

"Mom said that to her?"

"No, of course not. *I'm* just saying it to *you*. Jeez, Matt, I just said I didn't hear them say anything. You don't listen."

"Well, it's hard when you speak in a pitch only dogs can hear."

"Oh shut up…. It is super strange, though. Like what would those two have to talk about?"

Matt couldn't imagine what his mother and stepmother would be talking about if it weren't some misadventure of Julia's. And he could not picture his little sister hanging out at his mother's house. So, like most men of his age, he simply stopped trying.

"Yup."

"I mean not normal at all. Like super strange," Julia repeated as if to convey that Matthew was not responding adequately. "It's like Marilyn having tea with Jackie or something."

It annoyed Matt that his sister, who even he could admit was super bright, now seemed only capable of making references that involved celebrities. And her excessive use of the word "like" had started to give him a headache. She sounded like a moron.

"Yes, it is, like, crazy, psycho, insanely weird. Okay, I'm going to go."

"But don't you think it's …"

"I have to run, Mouse, I have class."

"Don't call me … Matt, it's Saturday. What class do you have on Saturday?"

"It's called introduction to I no longer care about this conversation."

"Oh ha ha. Screw you."

"Screw *you*," Matt replied, hoping to use it as his goodbye, but like the Energizer bunny, she just kept banging that drum.

"But it's weird, right?"

"Yes, like I said, really weird."

"Don't you want to know why she's here?"

"Are you going to go and ask?"

"Oh yeah, right, I'll just waltz in there and be like, 'what are you doing here?'"

"Well, get Ben to find out. She likes him."

"He's not here."

"Well then, wait till after and ask Mom."

"Seriously, Matt, I am going to go ask the mom about the stepmom. You are super dim sometimes."

"Says the straight-A student talking like reality TV star."

"Why are you so ... so, like, you don't even care about the drama going on downstairs? That is just like you Matt, so selfish. Just because you are away now, it's like you think don't even have to care about stuff any more. I don't know why you think it's so cool to be so, like, emotionally distant." Well, at least she still knew some big words.

"Okay, I have honestly not been paying attention to anything you've said in the last minute or so, and there is nothing that I can do about this situation, which is maybe none of our business, so and I'm going to hang up now. I know, screw me."

"No wait ... how can you say it's none ... oh never mind, I think I hear Ben. Maybe he'll be of some use. Okay, I'm going to talk to him about it. I'll keep you posted."

"Awesome."

"You're an ass."

"Bye."

Matt dropped the receiver and slumped back into his chair, exhausted. A phone call with his sister these days was like having a conversation with a chipmunk. And she really was getting dumber-sounding every time he talked to her.

"Who was that?" Matt's roommate called from the living room, without the slightest pretense that he hadn't been listening to the whole conversation. Privacy wasn't really an expectation one could hold in an apartment the size of a shoebox. But Matt had wanted to study on the west coast, so a shoebox was all he could afford. "Sounds serious."

"Nah, that's just the way we talk. She's all tweaked out because my stepmom's over at my mom's place." Matt would not normally have bothered to respond to Kevin's question, but he found himself wandering over to the door. As Julia had pointed out, *ad nauseum*, it was pretty weird.

"Oh damn, she in trouble?"

"No. I don't think so. She doesn't know. It's just a little odd since the two of them are not really friendly ... not even civil. The whole old wife, new wife thing, you know how it is."

In fact, Matt could count on one hand the number of times he'd ever seen them in the same room. Only at horribly awkward occasions, unfortunately tied to the major accomplishments in the lives of himself and his siblings. Graduation dinners or awards nights or big-digit birthday parties where everyone sat around uncomfortably and choked on superstore slab cake, while the kid in question smiled so hard their face ached, hoping to stave off the fight they assumed was boiling just under the surface. The last time would have been his high school graduation, over three years ago. The two had certainly never spent any time alone to his knowledge. And what the hell was Abby doing hanging out with his mother?

"Not really." Kevin broke into his train of thought. "My folks are still together. At least legally, I mean I don't know if they still you know ... oh gross ... oh no ... bad mental image." Kevin leaned forward, brought his fists to his eyes, and rubbed vigorously. Matt thought he might have lost his friend to the terror of imagining his middle-aged parents having sex, but Kevin recovered. "Ugh, that's worse than thinking about fatties doing it. So what'd you say was going on?"

"I don't know. I think they must be talking about my other sister. I have a younger one too ... little, my half-sister, I guess. Apparently she's been getting some kind of writing help from my mom."

"Weird."

"Yeah, apparently everyone thinks so."

"Though ... your mom's famous, right? Like, I mean Canadian famous?" Kevin asked.

Matt looked away out the window, unconsciously bringing his thumb to his mouth. "Well, not really, I mean she has a show on the radio and, like, wrote a book that won some stuff," he said, chewing aggressively on the skin around his nail. "I mean, it's on the public radio, it's not like Howard Stern or anything." Matt spat a little piece of skin on the tip of his tongue. He hated talking about his mother's work.

"Ummm, dude. We have talked about that. It's seriously gross," said Kevin, who seemed oblivious to that fact that he was living in a room that looked like a dump-site and smelled of mold, pot, and nacho cheese tortillas. Again, Matt thought he may have been successful in railroading the topic of conversation, but Kevin persevered.

"Too bad, Howard Stern is a genius, that would be cool.... A book too, eh? I didn't know that. So you're

going to be Just Like Mom then when you grow up?" Kevin
chuckled. He'd recently become addicted to watching
old game show clips on the Internet, and that one was a
current favourite.

This was why Matt hated talking about his mom. Not
that many young adult males were really into discussing
their mothers in any detail. But it was hard enough to be
a former jock turned Fine Arts major. His friends had been
making fun of him for it for years as they all went off to
study business or get into trades and actually tried to make a
living. But on top of that, he'd come to see that even when
he did manage to get some recognition for his work, which
had miraculously started to happen and was something he
knew he should be grateful for, he knew it was either never
going to measure up to what his mother did, or it would be
compared to it, or attributed to it. Who wants their work
constantly tied to their mother? But it was too hard for
people to resist — everyone loves a dynasty, even a barely
mediocre literary one. It was a hard pill to swallow, and he
wondered sometimes if it would sting so much if he were
competing with his dad. Because it *was* a competition, after
all, at least to him, and he suspected for her as well. So far
he'd never felt he had come even close to coming out ahead.

"Yeah, yeah, I can't wait for the cook-off," Matt said,
jerking his hand away and shoving it in his pocket, attempting
to sound bored. You couldn't tell a guy like Kevin to go to
hell, or you'd look like you cared. And if you cared, you
were done for.

Since Matt didn't rise to the bait, Kevin turned his
attention back once more to the conversation. "So it must
be a trip to have a real sister and a fake one, huh?"

"Well, she's not a fake one."

"Oh. I thought halvesies didn't really count."

"Of course they count."

"Yeah. Right. Sorry, I was thinking the step-ones. But still, they aren't the same, right?"

"I dunno."

Matt hadn't really thought about it before. He didn't often think about his siblings either. They were around or not around, and he didn't usually have a keen introspective interest about their relationships. He guessed he didn't really think of them as the same. They were so different, though they looked just the same — if you took a picture of Julia as a little kid, you were looking at Abby — but heaven help you if you told Julia that.

Plus, Abby was so much younger, and he had always gotten along with her. He had never blamed her for his dad leaving, or Jennifer either for that matter. As far as Matt was concerned, that debacle lay entirely at the feet of his father, though he'd stopped taking any real satisfaction in telling him so. It all seemed to have happened in another lifetime. And Abby was just a sweet, funny kid, and so, so smart. She really followed the beat in her own head, which he'd always been impressed by and encouraged. Never got sucked in to the stupid girl games and clothes and affectations that Julia had so willingly embraced. And Matt knew he was her favourite person in the world, which was kind of cool, though he wouldn't have admitted it.

As for Mouse, well, Jules and he had been fighting since birth. But he'd never let anyone talk trash about her. He'd fight them if they did, even if he agreed with them. Julia he liked in spite of herself. They were both his sisters, but Jules was family. He didn't know how to explain it. And when in doubt, avoid; life is just easier that way.

"I don't know, man. It's different but it's not. I don't really want to talk about it."

"Sure man, cool." The talk of game shows had stuck with Kevin and seemed to have had stolen what little attention span he had. His hands were already on the computer keyboard typing in a search on *Let's Make a Deal.*

"To be honest, unless she's hot and legal, I don't really care about anyone's sister.... Actually, how old did you say the older one was?"

"Go to hell, Kevin."

4

A S SOON AS CYNTHIA SAW THE LOOK ON ELLEN'S FACE, SHE knew it wasn't going to be an easy conversation.

She had avoided mention of her new little side project in the weeks since Abby had been coming over to the house after school. It was an arrangement made possible by a week of incessant pleading from Abby; a wealth of time and a lack of outside interests on Cynthia's part (along with some latent, probably unhealthy, desire to finger-poke the past); and a long and hard-fought debate between Tom and Jennifer in which Tom made excellent use of flattery, promises of increased time at home, a recommitment to seeing their couples therapist, and finally bribery to reach a successful end.

Cynthia had also been extremely amused and smugly satisfied to learn that Jennifer had been swayed by the chance to steal some time so she could explore a few slightly chemical enhancements to her inner and outer beauty away from the impressionable eyes of her daughter and the judgmental ones of her husband. A nervous Jennifer had shared the information herself minutes after knocking on Cynthia's door — either a nervous tic, or perhaps an offering accompanying her sincere and humbly presented request that Cynthia be kind to Abby, as she was a lovely little girl who might have crossed a boundary, but didn't know better and certainly didn't understand the repercussions.

Cynthia had read this, rightly, as a plea not to turn Jennifer into a villain at Abby's expense, and it moved her. She did understand the risk Jennifer was taking in allowing her daughter to get to know Cynthia, and realized the sting that must have come when Abby chose Cynthia as a mentor. Secretly, if not proudly, Cynthia took some pleasure in that fact, but she would never abuse it and told Jennifer so. It had been over a decade since the betrayal and the divorce, and while time may not heal all wounds ... it does dull the pain. It has to, or none of us would be functioning in any capacity. And she also understood the sacrifices a woman will make for her children. At one time it had been Cynthia spluttering and choking on her pride as she made nice to the new couple at Parents Night or the championship game.

The two women had even managed to get down a cup of tea during their conversation, even if they may have scalded their throats in an effort to drink it before the whole thing went ass over proverbial teakettle. Since then Jennifer had been wise enough not to return to the house, leaving Tom or Julia to deliver Abby to and from her lessons. So far they had been going pretty well.

But Cynthia hadn't found a way to tell Ellen about it. Over the course of several rounds on the picket line, post-protest drinks, and random phone calls, she had looked for an opportunity to casually mention it, but it never quite seemed a good time. Until the previous evening, when Cynthia, a bottle of wine to the good and riding high on the news that they all might be back to work by Thanksgiving, finally decided to run her little sociology experiment past the bullshit meter of her dearest and most opinionated friend.

On her first day on the job, almost twenty-five years ago, Cynthia had met Ellen in a series of humiliating stages. Cynthia had first noticed Ellen's shoes, pointed black snakeskin with elaborately engraved silver buckles. She'd had the chance to get a good look, on her knees, one bathroom stall over as she threw up the final remnants of her breakfast and wondered why she had ever left Ottawa to come to the big city. Next had come the voice, as loud as the shoes. "Hey, you dying in there? Cuz if it's just bulimia, pipe it down and let the rest of us crap in peace." Minutes later, as Cynthia cowered in the stall, too humiliated to be nervous any longer and waiting for everyone to leave, a hand had come under the stall door, bejewelled fingers with mustard yellow nails offering a wad of wet toilet paper.

"Hey, I was only kidding. And you are going to have to come of there eventually."

When Cynthia emerged, she was glad she'd had these initial glimpses because frankly, Ellen back in the day could really scare the hell out of you. Shaved head with huge pitch-black spiky bangs, nose ring, leather jacket, and blood red lips. As Cynthia took her in, feeling about twelve years old in her hot pink sweater and hoop earrings, Ellen continued. "So what's the deal? Pregnant?"

"No, just first-day-on-the-job jitters."

"You on camera or something?"

"Radio. I'm in arts programming."

"Ah, that's nothing to worry about then. Cheer up! You could be pregnant. I'm Ellen. I'm in the music department. Now let's get that vomit off your sweater and start creating us some Canadian culture."

For the next quarter century, rarely a day had passed when they didn't speak. Ellen had been there when Cynthia's vomiting had been child-induced, when the book came out and her career took off, when her marriage took the brunt of it and fell to shit. Ellen had been at times a more constant, if colourful stabilizing force in her kids' lives than either she or Tom could claim to have been. Less a surrogate parent or "auntie" than an eccentric and magical fairy godmother. She had always been there for Cynthia and always told her the truth, never one to hold back for the sake of pride or hurt feelings.

That night they had been rehashing some of the better times of their currently hiatused careers over the phone, Cynthia relaxing in the tub with a glass wine, when she decided to get it over with.

"You don't still have those snakeskin shoes, do you? I think you'd be able to get away with them on Queen Street today if you wanted."

"Do not be dissing my punk rock shoes, you wannabe Go-Go."

"No, no, I am all about nostalgia revisited these days," Cynthia said in a rather hairpin segue.

"Oh really? Do I sense a karaoke night in our future?"

"Perhaps, but I was actually talking about something a little more personal."

"Do tell."

Cynthia hesitated but knew that it was only a matter of time before Ellen heard about Abby from one of the kids. It had better come from her, or she'd look like she was hiding something. And she didn't have anything to hide. She didn't think so, anyway.

"I had a very unexpected visitor, well three actually, in recent weeks, and it's led to a rather unconventional way to pass my time."

"I said do tell. Ooooo, is it kinky?" Ellen said, not sounding too hopeful. She thought Cynthia was the least kinky person she knew, possibly the least on earth.

"No. It started with a drop-in from Tom's daughter, Abby."

"Le what?"

"Yeah, she came by here out of the blue one morning. That day I skipped out on the picketing."

"I should take the time to remind you what an ass you were for leaving me alone with Barney for an the entire shift, as it is universally agreed he is the worst, but I am intrigued, so I will let it go."

Joking, good, keep the mood light, Cynthia thought before plunging ahead. "You are too kind. Well, anyway, she came here to see if I would be a writing tutor for her, a sort of coach. Isn't that a gas? And it lead to a few surreal conversations with both her parents, including one with Jennifer alone, here at the house if you can believe it, and anyway I sort of said yes. So that's what I've been doing." She laughed through the ending, hoping to set a gentler tone for Ellen's rebuttal, and drained her glass. "How's that for kinky?"

"Oh, no. That's not kinky. Batshit crazy is what that is."

So, not joking any more then, Cynthia thought, dismayed to realize she'd left the bottle of wine on the bathroom sink.

"Well, no, I mean I know how odd it sounds but …"

"Trust me, Cyn. You have no idea how odd it sounds, or you would not be saying it."

"Just let me explain it."

"Oh, absolutely, but not tonight over the phone. I am too drunk for this right now. We will talk about this face-to-face tomorrow, and you will not be calling in sick, you got me?"

⟹•⟸

Ellen's dark, but lightly greying hair was now cut in a severe editor's bob, and she had replaced her leather jacket with a camel trench coat, but she looked no less intimidating as Cynthia walked up to the group assembled around a picnic table having their first coffee of the day. Ellen was standing with them, her dog Vicious, usually a bundle of nervous energy, standing docile at her feet, something he only did when Ellen was feeling under the weather. She had her sunglasses on even though the forecast called for rain. That was not a good sign.

"Grab a seat, Cyn, and give us your bet on when we'll be back in there," called one of her co-workers, a tall, lanky gambling addict who'd been running a number of pools since they'd been out. She wondered what he thought her odds would be of getting away without having to deal with Ellen when she was this hung over.

"Nah. Cynthia and I are going to take a little stroll."

"Not good," Cynthia mumbled, nodding hello and goodbye to the others, following obediently and taking a hold of Vicious's leash as Ellen grabbed two of the signs leaning against the table, handing one to Cynthia and using the other as a sort of cane.

They started the circuit in silence, Ellen's face unexpressive until Cynthia finally couldn't stand it any more.

"Okay, out with it."

"What is it you expect me to say?"

"Oh, I don't know. That I'm crazy, that I'm nosy, that I'm having some mid-life crisis. That I'm begging for trouble."

Ellen looked at her over the top of her shades, and Cynthia could see the eyes weren't unkind. "Well, that's a fair start. But honestly, what I really want to know is what you think you are getting out of this deal?"

"What do you mean?"

"Well, the kid is getting some free advice, and Tom is getting a chance to crawl back into the inner sanctum on her pigtails, and new wife's getting some free babysitting, though why she'd agree to leave her kid with you I do not understand, but whatever, that's between her and her therapist. I just want to know what's in it for you — a chance to screw with the new wife? An ego boost? A mini spy cuz your kids have stopped sharing the intimate details?"

"No!" Cynthia was deeply offended, but it was an unconvincing reply, and she knew it. Because, of course, it was a little of all of those things.

She couldn't remember the last time one of her kids had given a damn about anything she'd done for a living, except Matt, who'd spent their time together either trying to take her down a peg or distressed that he would never measure up and telling her to her face that she was out of touch, too jaded, and too comfortable to consider herself a writer any more. That all she did now was feed manufactured news to the masses who deserved better. This from a kid whose tuition she was paying. Of course, if she hadn't encouraged him to go to that school in the first place, he probably wouldn't be such a pompous ass ... and it wasn't like he didn't have a point.

And yes, damn her for it, but yes, the day that woman, that overly bleached and plucked and perfect woman showed up on her doorstep to tell her she would be willing to let Abigail work with Cynthia because the child had been despondent since she'd tried to shut it down, had been a great day. And to hear that Ms. Whole Foods was a pill-popping, face-peeling beauty junky. Oh, that was priceless.

It had been a salve for the still-lingering bruise of having her marriage so dramatically and publicly ended. It didn't fix anything, didn't change anything between them. But it had helped. And it was strange, but once Jennifer was in the house and they both realized it wasn't going to immediately burst into flames, Cynthia found it didn't hurt as much as she'd always imagined it would to have her there. Being in the power position for once helped, no doubt, but she also found empathy for this woman who was here to give her daughter all she wanted, even when what she wanted was for another woman to be her role model. Admitting that was a hard thing to do, and it was something Cynthia had been through. Julia had taken on a persona that was the antithesis of everything Cynthia would have chosen for her, and all Cynthia could do was support her or alienate her, because there was no way she could see of changing her mind.

It was also true that Cynthia liked hearing the little bits of family news that Abby let slip as they talked about writing from your life experiences. It wasn't spying, really, at least she wouldn't call it that. It was simply a way of glimpsing that part of her kid's lives cut off from her, something she had never expected would happen. She liked knowing that Ben's bedroom was green now and that Matt had called the other day to ask his dad to send his favourite sweater out because the weather was changing.

But she also really admired this plucky little kid trying so hard to be someone in the world. It was refreshing to be around someone with so much enthusiasm and energy to offer the process of creating herself, someone who didn't hesitate or bury herself in doubt. She really thought she could do anything.

"This kid, you have got to meet her, El, I mean she is really extraordinary. She is just so full of potential and so willing to throw herself into things. Plus she's funny. It's nice to see a girl not afraid to be who she is, you know?" She could tell from Ellen's face that she was explaining it badly.

"Honey, I know that Jules is being a real pain in your ass right now, but that doesn't mean you just pick up another one and start again. This is not your kid to mold."

Really badly.

"Wow. You think I don't know that? I of all people am certainly aware that that is *not* my kid. Trust me. And this is not about Julia. If someone asks you for a little help, and you have it to give, and it feels good to give it, why shouldn't you? It's nice to have somebody value your opinion. When's the last time any of my kids have asked me for anything other than money or to leave them alone?"

"Okay. Fine. So maybe the kids should not be your prime area of focus at the moment. They are not being anything other than kids growing up, you know. They are supposed to rip you to shreds right now. It's healthy. This is an opportunity for you, if you'd take it. A chance to worry a little less about helping kids get on with their lives and take a look at your own. I mean, why not take some of this free time and get into something that interests you, huh? Why get yourself involved in a family drama?"

Cynthia thought about this for a minute. She didn't like it, but it was a good point. Still, it ignored something that everybody always ignored, her chief among them, until a few weeks ago, but a nagging truth that was always present in her thoughts.

"Because we are *in* the family drama, Ellen. We've been in it for over a decade now. You think I'm not always thinking about them, aware of them? That the kids aren't always tip-toeing around us all watching what they say and so saying almost nothing. Ten years of stilted formal conversations with someone I used to love desperately — and who I once actually threw a kettle of boiling water at, and we've never once talked about it since? Don't you think I'm curious about this kid? About Tom's kid?"

In saying it out loud, shouting it really, she noticed some heads turning in their direction, and Cynthia felt a lightening, like a tension band had been suddenly cut loose from around her chest. She was never one to embrace what she thought of as weakness, or to dwell on the things she could not change. But she could admit that ignoring them had never made them go away, and it was nice to be able to say so.

"I don't know," she sighed, dropping her voice and waving at a few of the onlookers in an attempt to shame them back to their own conversations. "Maybe it's time we all stopped acting like we don't have anything to do with each other. We do. We so obviously do. Not talking about it hasn't solved anything, or fixed anything or made anything any better, has it? Maybe this kid is offering us all the chance to just try and live with it and see if it makes it any easier."

Ellen stopped walking and pushed her sunglasses on top of her head, a habit when she was thinking. Point Cynthia. After a solid minute, she spoke. "I have to tell you, this sounds like a bad TV movie in the making to me, honey.... But what the hell do I know? My most complicated relationship is with a miniature Schnauzer." She looked affectionately at the serious little face watching them, both ears alert, sensing the tension. "Well, except for you pack of loons," she added, picking up Vicious and tucking him under arm.

Cynthia smiled, touched by the gesture and her friend's concern. She really was one of the good ones, even with all her bluster.

"Who knows anything? I get that this is all unusual. And I see how it could end up being a really, really bad idea. I just think I have to let this play out a bit. It's like you said, the kids are getting older, and it's not like we have a lot of time to try and change things. If I don't do this now, then things just stay broken forever."

"I know that you are looking for something, and I hear what you are trying to do, but I don't want to see you get hurt."

"I know."

"And at the end of the day, if you really want to fix things, you are still going to have to figure yourself out, you know. The Cynthia part, too, not just this mom/ex-wife/workin' stiff character you've been rockin'."

"I know."

Ellen turned to face Cynthia dead on, looking hard into her eyes. "And please, please, please tell me — and don't lie to old Ellie now, because it's important we are both clear on this ... tell me you are not, in any way, thinking about this as some way to get back with that sack of shit ex-husband of yours, are you?"

Cynthia snorted and answered with absolute confidence. "Absolutely not."

Whatever it was that Cynthia was looking for, she knew for certain that it wasn't Tom. This wasn't about trying to become who they were before, which would be utterly impossible even if she wanted it, and she really didn't. Not any more. It was just about trying to become something a little better than they were now.

"I would swear it on my life, Ellen. I would even swear it on yours, and what the hell would I do without you telling me what to do all the time?"

Ellen snapped her sunglasses back down on her face, indicating that her sermon was over.

"Enough of this walking business, I feel as terrible as you look," Cynthia said, gently punching Ellen's arm to show all had been taken in the spirit with which it was intended, and that she really was grateful. They turned and headed back towards the picnic tables.

"If you end up crying even once over this, I will cut that man's nuts off … hers too."

5

THE WAY SHE WAS JUST STANDING THERE ALL ALONE, NOT
taunted or even shunned, just totally ignored, it could
break your heart ... until you saw the hat. A felt cloche
hat with a fur pom-pom on the side (ermine, she'd correct
you). This hat, on a ten-year-old, was just the icing on the
cake of the truly horrendous outfit Abby was sporting. A
cord skirt that went down past her knees, an old high-school
track shirt of Matt's, a sweater that would have suited a
librarian from the fifties, and a pair of Hello Kitty Mary-
Janes, and not ironic ones.

This is what Abby had chosen to wear during one of
the last days of a glorious Indian summer while all the other
girls in her class were still running around in glittery T-shirts
tucked into their brand-name skinny-legged jeans and their
cool shoes. All things that Abby had in her possession. Items
that less fortunate girls would sell their souls for completely
ignored, stuffed in her closet with the tags still attached,
while she ran around looking like a miniature senior citizen.

Then you sort of got it. The kid was a kook, and people, particularly pre-teen girls, do not like to hang around with kooks. Pre-teen girls of the new millennium do not want to talk about dead writers, or play-act at being horses, or Indian princesses, or fairies, and they don't walk around with their noses stuck in books, or wear bright purple backpacks with cartoon characters on them. Julia wouldn't talk to a kid like that either. To be honest, it was a miracle she wasn't bullied mercilessly, especially when she took on that snotty teacher tone of hers. Ignored was better than she should have hoped for.

Julia pulled the car up right in front of her, waited a moment for Abigail to lift her head from whatever bloated piece of literature she was pretending she could understand, and notice the car. When she didn't, Julia tapped the horn lightly, sending Abby into some kind of spasm that caused her to drop the book and tip over the unzipped schoolbag at her feet, spilling its contents all over the sidewalk. Abigail bent over quickly, and Julia saw her glance back to see if the cooler kids, who pretty much counted everyone but that kid who was sitting with a helper, had noticed. And of course they had noticed, laughing about it, tossing their hair as they did, in half-hearted attempts to pretend they were trying to hide it. *Just another nail in that coffin,* Julia thought, sighing impatiently and reflecting on how her brother had turned that kid into a grade-A geek and then sent her into the lion's den of middle school, leaving Julia to try and fix it, so far without much success.

But nobody else wanted to be the person who brought her down to earth a little bit, or to show her how to get along on it. Because Julia knew that what they don't tell you when they tuck you in at night and fill your head with notions about how great it is to just be yourself and how much better it is not to bow down to peer pressure or be untrue to yourself, is that it isn't easy, and it isn't any fun. The world is not kind to people who wave the individualist flag, so proud of themselves for being different, implying with their every action that they are somehow superior to the masses, those sheep going along with the flow.

Sure, it's fine to say it, maybe it's even true. But then you have to at least tell the kid how very lonely it will be to be so right all the time. How uninterested everyone is going to be in this wonderfully unique little person she is so graciously willing to share with them. How sorry they are going to feel for her walking around wearing her heart on her sleeve and offering herself up for their judgment when she is so clearly not playing by their rules. How amusing Abigail must be to them, how foolish she seems. Julia had learned it the hard way, and until she'd taken matters into her own hands, she too had spent her share of hours standing alone in the schoolyard. But she'd managed not only to learn how to play their games but master them, and now she was the one who got to decide who sat alone and who joined in. She was doing her best to show this to Abby, and surprisingly in the last few months had even gotten some support from Jennifer, who had also noticed that Abby spent far too much time either alone or chasing after her brothers. Now with Matt gone and Ben lost to hockey for the season, she was suffering.

But the girls didn't really get along. Seven was a lot of years between them, and it made it hard for Abby to keep up, and for Julia to remain patient, even after some of her anger and resentment had worn off about Abby existing in the first place. She'd been about as old as Abby was now when her dad left and Jennifer had entered her life. This beautiful, distant stepmother offering an endless stream of criticisms, commands, and beauty advice, and of course the new baby who Julia was meant to fawn over on weekends but remember not to talk about the rest of the time.

Abigail stuffed her belongings clumsily into the bag, keeping her head down as she did, and headed quickly for the car, looking up only as she grabbed the handle then stopped when she saw it was Julia in the driver's seat. Julia motioned for her to get in, indicating the door was unlocked, before rolling down the window.

"It's open. Get in."

"What are you doing here?"

"Cruising for eighth graders ... what do you think? Get in."

"Dad is supposed to come and get me."

"Your dad is working late and your mom is having some emergency meeting or something, so I have to take you to my mom's so you can have a writing lesson, because apparently I am only allowed to drive when it involves doing something totally lame and stupid. Now get in the car."

"Oh," said Abby, pleased about the lesson if not the means of transport, then adding, "He's your dad too." She shifted her bag from one arm to the other but still made no move for the door.

"Come on," Julia huffed, "everyone's looking at you." That got Abby into the car, but Julia regretted saying it. The kid looked sad, and as they drove away her eyes lingered on a group of girls sitting under a tree, heads close together as they turned threads of colourful string into braided friendship bracelets, their arms already bearing the load of previous work. Abigail pulled her sleeves down over her unadorned wrists, clutching the ratty wool in her hands.

Julia looked too and recognized a girl with bright red hair and a sea of freckles sprayed across her face as a kid that used to come to the house sometimes.

"Hey, isn't that your buddy, Freckles?" It was not Ben's most original nickname. He usually had quite a knack for it. He had some killer ones for Jennifer that even made their mom laugh.

"Her name's Sarah."

"Well, isn't that your friend Sarah?"

"Yes. No. She's not my friend."

"Well, you used to hang around with her all the time. I remember she could never go out on the slip 'n' slide because she'd burn so fast, and Jennifer was always so stressed about her, like, getting cancer."

"We are not friends any more."

"Why not?"

"Because she is stupid."

Of course she's stupid, she's ten, thought Julia but kept it to herself.

"Would you care to elaborate?"

"She only wants to play video games and talk about make-up and getting her ears pierced and the boys in our class, or the older boys," Abby said, rolling her eyes. "She only ever wants to hang out with the other girls now and never wants to do anything fun."

Pointless, this whole conversation was going to be totally pointless, thought Julia. But she'd seen the way Abby looked at those kids and knew she'd give her eyeteeth for one of those stupid string bracelets. Somewhere in the prematurely aging person beside her was a kid who would like being a kid if she could just figure out how to do it.

"Well, maybe hanging out with those other girls would be fun. Have you ever tried it?" Julia pressed.

"No," Abby said firmly, folding her arms across her chest. Julia reached out to turn up the stereo, figuring she'd done her best and the kid could just go on living the solitary life for all she cared. "They won't let me," Abby mumbled by way of explanation, and the volume came back down. Now they were getting somewhere.

"And why not?" Julia knew why not; she could give you a laundry list of reasons why not, but she needed the kid to acknowledge it. It was the first step in the process.

"Because they are stupid," came the petulant reply, followed by, "and they say I'm a weirdo."

Here was the opening Julia had been waiting for, and she seized it.

"Well, do you think maybe you *are* a bit of a weirdo?" asked Julia gently.

"No. I am just … different."

"There are those who might argue that different and weirdo are one and the same. So, just putting this out there, but maybe if you were a little less different, those girls would be up for playing with you sometimes. Like maybe if you put the book down every so often and came to school one day in something kind of cool and brought in one of those beading sets your mom is always buying for you, you could bring that to the table, you know? A little goodwill offering."

Abby looked at her disappointedly. This was just the kind of conversation she'd been having with her mother lately: Why don't you call so and so? I haven't seen so and so over here in a while, why don't you have a sleepover? And she didn't like it. When they started making ten-year-old girls that weren't stupid, boy-crazy idiots, then she'd start having sleepovers again. Until then, those girls weren't willing to bring any of her kind of goodwill to the schoolyard, why should she?

"Listen. I am not saying you shouldn't raid Matt's closet if that's your thing, or that you have to stop reading ridiculously grown-up books, or that you can't be as weird as you want to be. But just know that you are going to be doing it all by yourself, because regardless of what Matt or whoever may have told you, you can't expect to be accepted for it. That's bullshit."

"You swore," Abby said before she could help herself, then rushed to correct it. "I won't tell." They were always calling her a tattletale, so they never told her anything. And while she didn't like what she was hearing at the moment, there was something that seemed true about it, truer than what she'd been led to believe so far. "What do you mean?"

"Here's the thing, Abs, you can choose to be an individual and be all proud of yourself for that, or you can choose to give a little, and get along a little, and maybe not call everyone else idiots for liking the stuff they like, and you can maybe have a bit of fun while you're young, go to a party or two and get a boyfriend or something. Don't you want to have some friends?"

"Dad says people should like me the way I am," Abby countered, swaying ever so slightly but not wanting to be convinced without a fight.

"So you want Dad to be your only friend?"

"Matt liked books and reading. And he is smart."

"First, Matt is not the only one to get good grades, okay? And, I know you think he's Mr. Perfect, but he was also on the hockey team, remember? And he hung out with all the jocks at school, remember? You're wearing his track shirt right now, and *he* didn't even wear that to school. Trust me, all the reading the debating and the daydreaming he did, he did at home. Your dear Matt has a few swirlies on his conscience, don't think he doesn't … you know what a swirly is, don't you?"

Abby nodded, wide-eyed.

"Abs, you don't just get to walk around and be whoever you want to be at school. Not if you actually want anyone to like you."

"Is that why you act so dumb when you are talking on the phone?" Abby said, putting a hand over her mouth when she heard how it had come out. She didn't want to get Julia mad. Julia was really mean when she was mad. But Abby actually wanted to know.

"Excuse me?"

"I just mean how you laugh and talk about celebrities and everything … and about other kids at school," Abby said, her head down and eyes squeezed tight, waiting for the yelling to start, but Julia just snorted.

"Yeah. Yeah, maybe."

Abby could feel in her bones that it was probably better to stop while she was ahead, but she couldn't help herself. "But don't you want your friends to like you for who you are?"

"What, you mean the 'real' me?" Julia half-laughed, half-sighed. "I don't even know who the real me is. And frankly, most of them wouldn't deserve to know about it if I did. But you know what, it's fun to have people to hang out with and have a laugh with and kill some time."

"But when do you get to do the things you want to do and talk about the things you want to talk about?"

"That's what university's for," Julia said confidently.

She was counting on it. She had filled out the forms for the schools of her choice months ago, a choice largely based on schools as far away from home as possible, although Matt had already ruled out the west coast. She was certainly NOT going to end up following in that guy's footsteps ever again. "That's when you get to be the person you want to be ... I hope."

6

MATTHEW WAS NOT COMFORTABLE, BUT HE FELT ANCHORED to his seat, pinned by the eyes staring down at him from the walls of the lecture hall. Knowing eyes in pensive faces painted in oils and framed in gilt. Part of him wanted to make a run for it — he was practically in the back row anyway, steps from the door, but he remained uncomfortably in his seat.

"This is just such bullshit," he heard a voice mutter behind him, soft and feminine and exasperated. Matthew did not think he was meant to hear, though he agreed wholeheartedly. He wanted to believe he agreed wholeheartedly, at least. He thought he did, although he was not entirely sure what the voice was referring to. He had not been listening to the lecture.

Starting his fourth year two credits shy in his major, English, had led to some unfortunate class selections, and so now instead of taking a seminar course on Eastern Religions or an independent study option to work on his own writing, he was sitting with a horde of other students shoe-horned into a lecture hall receiving an introduction in children's literature. Although kiddie lit didn't seem to be the subject being discussed at the moment.

"There is no nobler pursuit than the acquisition of knowledge for the sake of knowledge," Matthew heard his professor say, leaning into the microphone for emphasis, his hands placed firmly on each side of the dais. He was a young-ish man, in his thirties, Matthew guessed, maybe early forties. He was dressed in a painfully cliché tan corduroy blazer, his hair in a state of messy perfection. Matthew thought he must use products to make it that way. From his vantage point he could see it was also thinning. Matthew used to be a goalie, and he had a good eye. All in all, it was not a look that he would be opposed to sporting one day, standing in front of a podium like that talking about books, though in his version the hair was thick and the audience smaller, leaning forward in anticipation of what he might say next, not tilted back unconscious.

"Yet, you sit there," the professor continued, "splayed out in your seats, and you massacre big fancy words or go to the pub and swill bad coffee or cheap beer, and drop names — a Nietzsche here, an Aristotle there, and let's not forget our Shakespeares and our Joyces — and you call yourselves students. But if all you want out of your education is a good school name to shove on your resume, some leg up on your career, then you shouldn't be here. You are wasting your time, and more importantly, you are wasting mine."

The room was hot. The lights and the combined body heat left the professor sweating, small dark circles visible under the arms of his coat when he raised his hands to rub his temples. "I am not here to teach the vain or greedy or lazy. If you are not here to learn, to embrace the subject matter at hand, to explore it passionately, then you do me, and all of us a grave disservice," he said plaintively, gesturing to the men lining the walls.

Through the humidity in the room, Matthew could smell the pine cleaner they used on the dark wood-panelled walls. On the rare occasions he'd made it to class early (to top it off, the course was set at the ungodly hour of nine a.m. on Fridays, as if a punishment geared towards those who had taken the class as their Hail Mary humanities credit or an easy A) he'd seen the women in their grey uniforms hunched at the waist as they rubbed it in, beads of oil bleeding into the lush green carpeting. He reached out to run a fingernail along a crack in the panelling, carving off fine curls of residue he watched float slowly to the ground before realizing he had made more work for those women, and stopped. Matthew decided the voice behind him was right.

"Such fucking bullshit," the woman repeated, louder this time, and Matthew felt the heat of her breath on his neck. Or thought he felt it. He sat up straighter, no longer listless, and tried to focus on what the man had just said that made her so upset. He looked down to see the thin-haired professor was watching him curiously, eager and unfriendly. Matthew instinctively minimized the YouTube video he had been playing on his laptop, even though it was not possible that the professor could see it.

"What's that?" the professor asked, still looking upward, head cocked as if somehow it would make it easier to hear from the back rows. Students turned in their chairs to stare openly, and Matthew's pulse began to race as he tried to calmly to meet the multiple gazes that had fallen upon him. His cheeks were now scarlet, and he strangled a cough while regretting he had not run out of this lecture hall when he'd had the chance, down the stone-arched corridors and back to the blessed solitude of his apartment.

"I said, with all due respect, Mr. Keillor, that this is fucking bullshit." The voice behind him was no longer soft, but smooth as velvet. Smooth as ice. It was the voice the professor was questioning, and the students shifted their collective gazes upward, eyes wider now, a mix amusement and astonishment. Matthew, once again gloriously invisible, thought he could kiss her in gratitude for this sweet relief. And then he decided he could also kiss her for the velvet voice and the breath on his neck and the way she said "fuck" to the professor. Matthew had become a new kind of uncomfortable.

"You would argue that is a respectful way to address a professor at a world-renowned university?" Keillor's hands were once again gripping the dais. His tone was one of mock incredulity, but those hands, Matthew thought, his hands gave him away. The dude was pissed.

"I said it with all the respect that was due." Her voice again, her breath. Matthew was now certain he had felt it against his scalp, through his close-cropped hair. A hockey haircut, his father called it. *Nobody's going to get a hold of you under the helmet with a haircut like that.*

"And correct me if I'm wrong, but isn't your title *Assistant Professor?*"

The woman had leaned forward, her mouth now closer to Matthew's ear. She was chewing cinnamon gum, and Matthew thanked the god of his still-recent youth for the cover of his laptop. Too stunned to turn around at first, he realized it was now too late to take a look at this cinnamon-scented goddess. The other students were all facing forward again, eyes on their laptops. The show had taken a step too far into the uncomfortable, and they no longer had any desire to be a part of it. So, with no other option, Matthew just pushed himself as far back into the plush seat as he could in a token sign of solidarity and hoped she would continue. And she did.

"Either way, I don't have much respect for a man standing there judging my motives and my integrity and spewing elite garbage about an institution that has loaded so many students in here that I can't even see the PowerPoint slides you've slapped up there to tell me how pathetic I am."

As she spoke, Matthew cleared his screen and fiddled with the angle in a vain attempt to catch her reflection in it. Although it really didn't matter what she looked like at this point, Matthew was already certain that he was in love with her. At least he definitely wanted to have sex with her. Even if she wasn't as gorgeous as he now believed her to be. Matthew would probably not have said no to the chance at having sex with any girl, but especially one who could talk like that.

He could see, even from the back of the hall, that Keillor's face was now mottled with rage. Then, with swift steps, the professor made it halfway up the aisle before an errant school bag strap caught his foot, forcing his arms into a frantic windmill, which though graceless, made successful his attempt to stay upright. It did nothing to improve his mood. The room was silent until, with as much dignity as he could muster, he said, "Just who the hell do you think you are? Hmmm. Tell me, what is your name?"

"My name? Well, I guess that's the one upside to this whole impersonal farce you call a world-class educational experience. Halfway into the semester and my professor doesn't know my name. And not another person in this auditorium full of people does either."

But Matthew wanted to. He wanted her. He wanted her so badly that even with the professor staring down at her, still furious, he found himself no longer able to stand not knowing what she looked like. Even the unwarranted mortification he'd been feeling a few minutes earlier, which had been considerable, had not been able to dampen his arousal. He sat, cheeks still flushed and computer still firmly planted on his lap to contain its physical personification, and wondered if the shame and fear hadn't actually turned him on more. As a young man whose sexual history was much less interesting than that which might normally be attributed to a good-looking high school jock, the idea that being publicly humiliated could be kinda hot was one of the pervy-est thoughts Matt had ever considered. Until he realized he was sitting there thinking kinky things in a room full of people, with a boner pressing against his jeans, and that seemed even kinkier. At that point he knew that whatever happened between he and the girl with that voice, it was already the sexiest relationship he'd ever been in.

So he turned around. She was nothing like he'd imagined. She was no vixen, no temptress, no Joan of Arc. She was just an average girl, pretty though. Pretty in the way that plain girls can be when they are angry or elated, with a sparkle in their eye and the colour high in their cheeks. It was more than enough. She was perfect.

"Hi, I'm Matthew," he said, almost without thinking and breaking the nervous tension of one hundred students, released in a long peal of laughter which almost drowned Assistant Professor Keillor's wish that they would all "Go fuckin' fuck yourselves," before he turned on his heel back towards the safety of his podium.

As he fumbled angrily with his belongings, the students gathered their things and beat a surprisingly hasty retreat, considering their numbers. The woman didn't move. She was looking at Matthew, who was still looking at her. He had never done anything like that before, his dark good looks and sports credibility having done a wonderful job of covering his intense shyness around women, and now he had no idea what to do next. Her expression wasn't exactly hostile, he didn't think ... but the look on her face did manage to quell the fire in his cheeks ... and nether regions. In the absence of anything better coming to mind, Matt continued to look at her in silence.

Turning back around now seemed ridiculous, and he already knew he was not going to leave before her. She was still staring but said nothing. Matthew wondered if she was angry that he had lightened the mood, making her statement seem a bit of a joke. Or maybe she was glad that he had ended the standoff before some fear of repercussion or humiliation caused her do it herself. Possibly she was just happy to have a name to put to on face in this giant group of strangers. She kept looking at him, seemingly waiting for something.

"Hi, I'm Matthew," he said again. "What's your name?"

"Britney," she said, "and please do not say 'oh, like Spears,' because then I will just have to punch you right in the face."

"Fair enough. Perhaps we should get out of here, Britney, before you get punched in the face, academically speaking?" Matthew said, trying to sound cool and not quite hitting the mark, and in that, unbeknownst to him, hitting it perfectly.

"Good idea. Though now that he's short-shifted us on class time, I have about three hours to kill before my next class."

The opening was kindly obvious, and Matthew took it.

7

THE STEADY DRONE FROM THE CLASSROOM VENTILATION system drove her to distraction most days. But this was not most days. Today the continuous noise offered a welcome relief, camouflaging the sound of her pencil on the paper, the drumming of his expectant fingers as he waited for her response, the sound of her heart pounding as if trying to remove itself from her ribcage entirely and hop across the aisle into his waiting hand.

Looking up, Julia scanned the room nervously, finding it almost unfathomable that the rest of the class remained unaware of what she was about to commit to this very weekend. And not just a verbal agreement either, this was now on paper. She was finalizing the arrangements for a monumental, possibly life-changing event. This was going to be a weekend that she would tell her children and grandchildren about. Well, the women. When they were older. When it was not too creepy. Or maybe not. It certainly wasn't something she had gone enquiring of her own mother. Gross. Whatever, it was certainly something she would be telling her friends.

Leah was looking over expectantly, flashing her the horns before tossing a nervous glance towards the front of the room. Leah was Julia's best friend. She was an actual friend, not a frenemy, and had been intimately involved in the rituals and negotiations that had been undertaken up to this point. Leah knew what was at stake. She turned back once more to wink, smile, and make a filthy gesture before dropping her head into her hands and trying to focus on Twentieth-Century Europe.

Julia wondered for the millionth time if she was ready for this. She looked over at Jesse, who was watching her out of the corner of his eye. She could see his slight blush, the tension in his ropy arms — basketball player's arms. She knew he wanted an answer. And she knew this might be her last chance to give it to him. He turned a quarter inch in his chair, raising his eyebrows pointedly toward the square of crumpled looseleaf paper sitting in her lap where he had managed to land it minutes earlier. He had laid all of his cards on the table.

All the weeks of pushing and pleading and teasing and making out in front of the lockers had led to this one question and this one chance to move their budding relationship to the next level, not to mention her status at school. She was one of the last virgins left in her group. It hadn't gone unnoticed.

She knew she was physically ready. She'd seen the health class charts and read the pamphlets her mother slid under her bedroom door one sunny Saturday shortly after she got her period, hilariously the same ones her stepmother had left on her bed around the same time. And she liked Jesse, she was pretty sure about that. And he had been wholeheartedly endorsed by Leah, Molly, and Diana via a flurry of intricately folded and stealthily delivered notes, not to mention a full week's part-time pay in texting fees. She thought he was hot too. Everyone thought Jesse was hot. She knew her friends were suitably jealous; she'd seen the one too many photos of him on Diana's computer.

And, as of 2:15 p.m. today, she knew officially that he liked her back, at least enough to want to sleep with. He'd affirmed it with the request he sent sailing across the wide puce-colored aisle between them.

"What's it gonna B grrrrl. Yes or no? What's it gonna B grrrrl Yes or No? J."

Jesse had been listening to a lot of classic rock of late, eschewing the iPod for his parents' "vintage" record collection. So she knew she also thought he was pretty cool, though she couldn't help laugh when she saw he'd signed it. Like, he'd just thrown it at her, she was pretty sure it had come from him. So he wasn't the brightest. So what?

Molly had been rhythmically kicking her chair while she wrote. Having been left out of some of the key conversations regarding the doing of this particular deed, a punishment for some stupid thing she'd said, or done, or worn, Julia couldn't remember at the moment, Molly had only today realized how quickly things were proceeding. While normally this action would have driven Julia to a code red annoyance level, today it was soothing to know that someone else was also keyed up about the message, which she had now replied to, having in the preceding five minutes once again weighed all possible consequences and crafted her response.

Yes ♥

She had pencilled in a heart beside it as a compromise to the idea of writing *I Love You*.

Did she love him? She had no idea. But while she'd never consider herself a priss or anything, she did think it was something you should say to someone you were going to let see your bits. Still, actually putting that down on paper was even scarier to her than some of the advice she'd heard from within her circle about prepping for the big event. Everything from bringing a gallon of lubricant, to getting some practice in with a dildo or closest available facsimile, to getting drunk off her ass so as to avoid feeling any discomfort.

With one last encouraging look from Leah, Julia folded the note up into a teeny triangle and caught Jesse's eye. He turned, and seeing the note in her hand, sat up a little straighter, and shook his head slightly. They both knew that her throwing skills were nowhere near good enough to land it anywhere near his desk. And this was certainly not the sort of message intended for anyone but the two of them ... and all of her friends ... and maybe two of his.

He leaned out into the aisle ever so slowly, and she followed suit, watching for the slightest sign the teacher was onto them. Just as she entered into passing range, Molly's ballpoint pen hit the floor and heads began turning.

"Sorry," she whispered, a little too loudly.

Jesse's reaction was swift and he was back in position in a flash, eyes glued to the board. If everyone else hadn't now been looking the other way, he'd be the very picture of an attentive student. Julia had frozen into position and stopped breathing, her hand extended to no one, the little triangle of paper glowing in the overhead fluorescent light, catching the teacher's eye. Julia was called up to the front of the class and asked to hand the note over. The teacher took the triangle from Julia's trembling hand, tossing it lightly up in down in her palm, and watched the colour drain out of

Julia's face, which she had vainly attempted to arrange into a look of bored ambivalence.

"Is this a personal note, Ms. Wilkes?"

"Yes."

"Yes what?"

"Yes, Mrs. Segal."

"And you would like to keep it a personal note?"

"Yes, Mrs. Segal."

"Yes what, Mrs. Segal?"

"Yes please, Mrs. Segal," Julia said, more pleading than she would have liked in front of all her classmates, but now was not the time for insolence, and she knew it.

"Then may I suggest in future you not bandy such notes about in my class," Mrs. Segal said, flicking the note back at Julia, who grabbed it and shoved it deep into the pocket of her jeans.

"Eyes on your books, everyone," Segal called out as Julia walked swiftly back to her desk, looking quickly to Leah, who was sending her sympathetic looks and mouthing "that bitch," nodding in Molly's direction. But Julia wasn't worried about Molly now; in fact, she might even have to thank her for this, because all Julia could see at the moment was the smirk on Jesse's face as he stared down at his textbook, not even bothering to catch her eye.

Julia did not look up from her book again for the duration of the class and was the first one out the door when the bell rang, the note still tucked inside her pocket, where she decided it was going to remain for the foreseeable future.

She had always felt that any trust you put into a man had to be of the sort you'd be willing to throw away, but she had hoped that she was wrong. To be so careful all of the time was exhausting, and it certainly didn't help your reputation in high school. She wanted so desperately to be carefree and to have the fun everybody else seemed to be having, but she had always pulled back at the last minute. They just always seemed to let you down.

She genuinely didn't understand how people could function as half of someone else, how her friends could just so easily throw themselves into the arms of someone almost guaranteed to turn out to be a jerk, and then after a suitable two-week mourning period gear up to do it again. How they could be so enthusiastic about the opportunity to let somebody make you feel so stupid, so wrong? She was seething now, humiliated. Mad at herself, and furious with Jesse, who she knew was trying to catch up with her down the hallway. She sped up and turned a corner, almost hitting Leah, who was standing with her wallet in hand, head on.

"So I would guess that we are now heading for some retail therapy?" she asked before linking arms with Julia and pulling her quickly down the hall and out a side entrance. "Move it, Jules, if I get caught skipping out again, I'm gonna be like, excommunicated or something."

"You don't have to do this," Julia said, though she kept walking. "It's no big thing, I'm fine."

"Oh, we are going all right. I saw Jesse throw you under that bus, stupid asshole. But girl, it's like you always say, when something bad happens to you, you get to have something good happen to you. In this case, public humiliation and jackass boyfriend equals new jeans. And I, as your best friend, am, like, duty-bound to escort you. Plus I myself am also a fan of new jeans. So let's roll." Leah winked and ran ahead, taking off around the corner, and Julia followed, thinking how very few people there are that you can really count on in life.

8

"Morning, Cynthia."

"Morning, Carol."

"Welcome back? Is that what the hell I'm supposed to say?" her boss asked sheepishly as they got into the elevator together on her first day back at the office.

They had both just finished listening to a trio of their higher-ups address all staff in a cautious and most certainly lawyer-vetted presentation aimed at pumping some inspiration into the newly returned employees as they embarked on bringing the organization up to full operational speed, knowing that they were doing it with less staff and less financial security than they had before. It was accepted without complaint by a stone-faced crowd who had held their noses and listened more gratefully than they would ever admit for the reinstatement of a steady paycheque, while the rest of the management team stood off to the sides, smiles firmly planted on their faces and applauding politely to kill the silence that had followed the speeches.

Soon after, everyone had headed for the normalcy of their workstations, leaving the welcome-back coffee and muffins almost untouched, an almost unheard-of occurrence.

It had been an awkward, heated time, and lots of people had said lots of things they sorely regretted now that the "lazy, overpaid Communists" and the "evil, money-grubbing dictators" had morphed almost overnight back into the work colleagues they had been two and a half months before.

"It'll do in a pinch," Cynthia said, offering a charitable smile. In the end it was all just business, emotionally devastating and soul-crushing business, but they were going to have to bury their hatchets someplace other than each other's backs if the place was ever going to be bearable again. Might as well do it right off the bat.

It was easier for Cynthia to say than most she knew. Her job had remained unchanged, and no one was in a position to angle to take it from her. That wasn't the case for most, not even for Ellen, who was still waiting to see what a new spate of layoffs was going to mean to her recent promotion. She had enough seniority to keep her job, of course, over twenty-five years at the corp. But whether it was the job she'd signed on for remained to be seen.

When they arrived on the floor, Carol made a hasty exit to her office after murmuring a quick hello to the other staff members who were gathered around a desk engaged in an adult version of "What I did on my Summer Vacation."

"Oh, don't get me wrong," Stephanie, one of the producers, was saying, "we paid for it. Financially we are just about screwed, and Jack's education fund is now basically a stack of scratch tickets … but man, the time to myself … to finally have the chance to change my damn bedroom curtains and go see some matinees. I can't say I regret it. Whatever brought it on."

"What about you, Cyn," someone asked, noticing her arrival. "What did you do on your Social Service Sabbatical?"

"Nothing much. Dreaded the picket line and watched a lot of bad daytime TV. I for one am glad to be back."

That was the truth. After the novelty of Abigail's introduction into her life, things had settled back into the same tired old routine. Even though the visits with the girl were still entertaining, they only accounted for an hour or two every week, and that left an awful lot of time to fill. The kids were in school and had begun to stay out later during the evenings because of activities and friends and romances, and also, Cynthia feared, an aversion to how anxiously she had begun to await their arrival home so she could hear a voice other than her own or Oprah Winfrey's.

"Seriously?" said Gary, an old friend she had not seen once on the picket line and who, rumour had it, had forgone the strike pay for the chance to get a preview of his impending retirement spending his days touring around Toronto Harbour on his sailboat.

"Unfortunate as the cause was, kiddo," Gary called everyone kiddo, "that was a golden opportunity. I mean, unless you are planning on writing another Canadian bestseller and those hundreds in residuals start pouring in, when do you think you're going to have another shot at that kind of uninterrupted free daylight time to manage how you like? When you are too old to enjoy it, that's when."

"Wow. Thanks for sugar-coating it, Gary," Cynthia said, dropping her bag on the floor and feeling all of a sudden like this was the last place she wanted to be.

"Sorry, sorry all. I'm just saying that it sucks that we are trained so long in these routines, coffee in the a.m., something to eat at noon, watching the news at six or eleven. We're going to be 'working' through our retirements, if we can afford to have them at all. Always tied to the friggin' clock. Too tired to do all the stuff we've been putting off doing until we have the time. So it's too bad you all didn't take advantage of this chance to live a little."

"Well, some of us actually wanted to support our union," said another old-timer, a notorious workhorse who'd been sitting off from the others at his desk, already catching up on weeks of missed email. "Besides, it's hard for some people to just sit around with their thumbs up their keesters when they are the job. You wouldn't understand it, Captain No-show, but Cyn's like me, she's the job. Right, Cyn?"

No one was paying him any notice; he also had the reputation of being an angry old coot. For her part, Cynthia just smiled. "Right you are, Barney," she said, picked up her bag, and made her way to her office. She closed the door and the blinds, sat at her desk, turned on the computer, then dropped her head down on the desk.

It was true, she *was* the job. It was often she who turned on the office lights in the morning and shut them off again at night. Cynthia who ordered the kids pizza from the office because she wasn't going to make it home in time to cook them something, or eat it with them. And more often than she'd like, now that she thought about it, it was Ellen who dropped the kids off at hockey, or dancing, or had them for sleepovers, because Cynthia had gotten herself some speaking engagement or charity event appearance.

There wasn't really anything wrong with being the job. If she were a man, no one would even think twice about it. As a single mom, some might even say she should be admired for providing so well for the kids. Plus she didn't think it had really done them any damage. They were independent spirits — she'd raised them to be, and she never missed out on a recital or awards presentation. None of the memory moments.

The problem was just that Cynthia had never intended to be the job. It was one thing to be that way because of an overriding passion, a sense of duty or purpose, even a compulsive personality flaw. Cynthia had none of those reasons — in fact, she was having the unhinging thought that she'd not even known she *was* the job until Barney had so innocently pointed it out, and no one had thought to disagree with him. He was right, but it was in the absence of her being anything else. It had happened by default. How pathetic was she that the thing she spent the majority of her time doing was something she didn't even really care about?

Not the writing, never the writing. That she loved. Or had. She hardly did it any more, acquiescing to the producers and researchers in that department in lieu of the mechanical elements of the job. The phoning and planning and scheduling and glad-handing authors who, at least to her face, considered her a peer. Sometimes, and she hated to admit this, though why stop the self-confessing now, she relied on just showing up somewhere and letting her past opinion and articulations carry her through the numerous and forgettable fundraising dinners or conference panels or the like.

At home the situation was even more desperate. The "writer" hadn't picked up a pen in almost two years to set towards anything guided by the heart. In fact, she was hardly even reading any more. She didn't really cook, she bought her garden flowers already in bloom from the nearest tool superstore, she hadn't come in contact with a piece of sporting equipment that didn't belong to one of her children in years. She gave money instead of time to the causes that she held dear, arguing that she didn't have the "time" because there was always something to do at work, and she certainly didn't have a friggin' sailboat.

Ellen was right, her kids were right, the snotty little know-it-alls. Cynthia was a woman without a cause, without a plan, without a future. She would be left alone one day to stare at her dusty old awards and her thirty-five-year company pin, drinking boxed wine out of a coffee mug and guilting her children into spending long, boring afternoons sitting uncomfortably on her couch while she repeatedly told them how her life had been stolen from her. How she coulda been a contenda. It was really all too much to bear this early on a Monday morning.

She sat there unmoving, head low, spirits lower, until Ellen, without feeling the necessity of knocking, popped her head in the door.

"That good being back, huh?" she said. Cynthia simply moaned in response.

"What's the problem, honey? They say you were going to have to meet with an efficiency consultant to review your budget too? Can't keep all our technicians employed, but they managed to save up enough for an efficiency consultant. This place is a nightmare I just can't seem to wake up from." Ellen dropped into a chair and stamped her Blundstone-clad feet in anger. "Dammit dammit dammit. I think I'm going to lose the damn show. Wind up my days as a customer service rep or some shit."

Cynthia snapped her head up from the desk, immediately unable to tolerate the indulgence of her self-pity in the presence of such an actual injustice. Ellen looked defeated, and that wasn't like her. She was so convincing in her role as post-modern warrior-princess that Cynthia sometimes forgot she was real people. "Are you serious, Ellie? God, I'm so sorry. No, I didn't hear anything like that. My problem is self-inflicted and self-centred, as is my way."

Cynthia offered a brief recap of what had transpired that morning, still feeling the sick flutter in her stomach, even though she knew her problems were nothing in comparison to what her best friend and many of her colleagues were facing. "So I am just sitting here in my cozy office wondering what the hell I'm going to do with my life, like a jackass."

Ellen looked at her hard for a moment before grinning a little as she leaned forward. "Well, in that case you don't need to be worried about your future. There's always a solid demand for jackasses around here." That set them both off in a fit of laughter so hard and so long that when Gary finally popped his head in the door to find out "what was so damn funny," they were both red-faced and wheezing.

"Nothing," said Ellen after she managed to catch her breath. "I simply and wholeheartedly endorse your 'living life in the moment' philosophy there, Gar. And I'm guessing those weasels have slunk back to their caves, or wherever the hell weasels live, by now, so why don't you and me and miss workaholic over here waste a little more of that dwindling taxpayer money and head on down to grab some of those blood muffins. I think we've earned them."

9

"SO WHAT DO YOU CALL HER?" SARAH ASKED, STRETCHING her arms over her head and wiggling her toes under the duvet she and Abby were sharing.

"Cynthia." Abby said it like it was no big deal. "She's cool about it."

Abby's friendship fortunes had changed significantly since the facts-of-life talk she'd had with her sister. First, she had agreed to wearing jeans to school now that the weather was getting a little colder, a brand heartily endorsed by the tween fashion experts at her school. Her mother was so thrilled, a shopping trip was planned to make sure that Abigail Wilkes was now known for having the newest and the best fall fashions in school.

Second, her ex-friend Sarah had come to class one day suffering from a flu bug and had, to her ultimate humiliation, thrown up. Not at her desk or anything — she'd made it to the bathroom, but it hadn't taken long for news to spread along with the nickname "Sarah Spew," making her the social pariah of the month and so much more than open to Abby's clumsy advances in the yard at recess. Finally, Abby had let it be known to Sarah, who had passed it on to the other girls, gossip being a key way to buy back status, that she was now hanging out with someone kind of famous, her dad's ex-wife. Abby had gone from eccentric to interesting overnight.

"Couldn't have played that better myself," Julia had congratulated her when she noticed the change in apparel and the fact that occasionally when the phone rang at her dad's place, it wasn't for her.

Abby had been building momentum, first a few words in the schoolyard, then hanging out after school, and she had just landed her first sleepover guest. Two, actually. Sarah, and Emma Stevenson, commonly held to be the coolest girl in fifth grade. Jennifer had been so pleased to hear about it, she'd even broken down and picked the girls up some junk food ... including Pop Tarts. Abby had to admit there were some perks to this going-with-the-flow philosophy.

"Have you gone to see her work yet?" Emma asked from her sleeping bag on the other couch. This had never actually come up, and now that Cynthia had gone back to work, they weren't really meeting any more, but Abby wasn't about to let that slip.

"Not yet. Soon."

"Awesome. Maybe you'll see a famous person."

"Yeah, probably," Abigail said the offhand manner that she heard Julia use on the phone so often.

"Ooooh, like who?" said Sarah, perking up.

"Ummmm, Peter Mansbridge?"

"Who?"

"Never mind...."

"Still," said Emma, unconcerned with the details. "It's cool."

"Yeah, cool," Sarah chimed in.

"Cool."

The conversation wasn't outstanding, but Abby was committed to staying quiet and following their lead. It had been working so far.

Emma had just put in her request for autographs when Abby saw Ben come into the room, and shushed them all fiercely. This wasn't something she wanted him overhearing, since she knew she wasn't painting a true picture, which left her vulnerable to some embarrassing teasing should Ben seize the opportunity. And he almost always did. But the other girls had already stopped talking, their attention now focused on Ben, giggling as they pulled their blankets up to their chins.

"Good morning, Ben," Sarah called out, taking pleasure and full advantage in her status as first friend.

"Yo, G-Abby, Freckles … other kid," Ben said with a nod on his way through to the kitchen, sending the girls into a fit of laughter.

"Oh, your brother is SO funny!"

"And he is SO cute," Emma chimed in.

"Gross," Abby replied. She couldn't possibly be expected to have to go along with people talking about how cute her brother was, could she? Well, she wouldn't. It was just too gross.

"Abbeeee, how come you didn't. tell us he would be here? I am like, sooooo embarrassed," Emma scolded, not looking the least bit embarrassed as far as Abigail could tell. "And I'm sitting here in a Barbie sleeping bag like a baby."

"He doesn't care," Abby said.

"Oh, what do you know? Does he have a girlfriend? I bet he has a girlfriend," Emma said sadly, jumping out of the bag and folding it twice to hide the offending pattern.

"How could he not? He's soooo sexy," Sarah piped in, blushing and stumbling a bit as she tried to say it with conviction. Much like trying to look elegant the first time a girl slides on a pair of high heels.

Desperate to get off the subject of her brother, who she knew could overhear them and was certain to tease her mercilessly for all of the giggling and her part in it, Abby said, "Forget him. What do you want to do? Want to go and try on some of my clothes?" They had spent more time last night than Abby would have thought possible trying on her clothes, but it seemed to have been a big hit with the other two, and it would at least get them out of the living room.

"Been there, done that," said Sarah, then, after thinking for a moment, "but I would like to go try on some of Julia's clothes."

"Ooooh, that's the older sister, right? Yeah, let's go see her clothes," chimed in Emma, dress-up having not having yet been fully superceded by boy-chasing in her pre-pubescent mind.

That was *not* a possibility, and Abby knew she had to nip this line of thinking in the bud, but wasn't sure how. "Ummmm, we can't."

"Why not?"

Abby was trying to find a cool way of saying she was not allowed in Julia's room. Ever. But before she could come up with one, Emma cut her off.

"She's not here, is she?"

"Um no ... but Ben would tell," Abby said seconds before she heard Ben shout, "Dad, if we are going to make it to this practice, we need to leave now," before closing the door behind him. Abby was abandoned in her argument.

"Well, that takes care of Ben," said Sarah, gleefully tossing off the comforter and racing up the stairs with Emma in hot pursuit, leaving Abby no choice but to follow, a sense of doom mounting. They passed her father on the stairs, and when he stopped to wish them all a good morning, Abby almost told them what they were up, to hoping he could make it stop and save her from probable murder once Julia found out they'd gone through her things, but she couldn't get the words out and stood mute as he ruffled her hair, told them to be good, and ran out after Ben.

Opening the door to Julia's room, Sarah and Emma let out a collective sigh. Even as a secondary residence, Julia had set the place up in style. Fashion magazines littered the desk, along with an impressive assortment of make-up and accessories. In her beautiful handwriting she had painstakingly copied out the lyrics to her favourite song on the wall above her bed, something Jennifer had yet to forgive her for. Scattered across the bed, the chair, and the window seat were clothes. The girls were in heaven, at least two of them.

Though Abby often longed for this kind of opportunity and sometimes took advantage of Julia's absences for the tiniest of peeks inside, she regarded with total panic the two whirling dervishes already wreaking havoc and making no attempt to put things back where they'd found them.

"Oh. Oh. Oh. Please no. Don't touch anything. Let's ummmm, let's go do something else? Do you want a Pop Tart?" Abby pleaded, ditching all efforts to try and be cool, as her friends set about the room grabbing scarves, holding up earrings. They seemed to be everywhere at once.

Knowing she'd lost them to the seduction of teenage ephemera, she could only attempt to instruct them to respect the rules of successful snooping. Whispering "Put the earrings back on the table," "That shirt was on the floor," so that her mother, cooking breakfast downstairs, wouldn't hear them.

"Don't be such a baby, Abby. The place is a mess, it's not like she's going to notice," Emma said.

Abby had noticed that Emma was kind of a bully, and she didn't ever take no for an answer, so Abby just stood by the doorway, listening for footsteps and shhhh-ing incessantly as she memorized where everything had started in the vain hope that she might be able to put some of it back.

"Wow. You should try and borrow some of this stuff, Abby," Emma continued at full volume. "These jeans are sick. I can't wait until I get some hips," she said, holding them in front of her at the mirror, where she saw Jennifer's reflection and dropped them like they were on fire.

"What are you girls doing in here?" Jennifer said, ending the fashion show, to Abby's overwhelming relief.

"Oh. Hi, Mrs. Wilkes," Emma said, offering her most charming dance-school smile. "Abby said we could."

So she's a liar too, Abby thought.

"Well, Abby was mistaken," Jennifer said, grabbing the sweater that Sarah, who had frozen when Jennifer entered the room, had halfway over her head, and ushering them all out of the room.

"Go downstairs now and eat your breakfast. Abigail, we are going to have a talk about this." Jennifer had spoken sternly to try and exhibit some kind of parental authority, though from the panicked look she'd seen on Abby's face when she walked in, she knew there was no chance that this had been Abby's idea.

Jennifer folded the sweater and placed it on the bed then wearily scanned the chaos. She mindlessly picked up the jeans left by Emma, and as she folded them in a vain battle against the mess, she noticed a piece of paper had tumbled out. She picked it up to shove it back in the pocket but stopped, drawn to the intricate folding that gave it away as a personal note. Jennifer used to write notes like that. A wave of nostalgia washed over her as she ran her finger along one side, loosening the fold that held the note closed, then sat down on the corner of the bed and opened it up, mildly curious.

Julia guarded her personal life like a crypt-keeper — you never had any idea what she and her friends were really up to. It was too tempting to resist, so Jennifer gave in, thinking the worst she'd see was that Julia thought she was a bitch, which wouldn't have surprised her. She regretted it immediately. As her eyes scanned the page, even with her limited knowledge of music, she immediately registered the lyrics scrawled in the hand of a boy obviously raised on computers, and knew what they were intended to convey. Then she saw the response, and the carefully drawn heart, and she really, really wished she hadn't picked up the damn jeans.

So Julia was seeing someone. Or at least she was having sex. Wow. Of course, the girl was seventeen, it wasn't like this shouldn't have been on the radar, but Jennifer had never really had to think about it. It was one of very few upsides to the role of stepmom. Aside from sharing a few very basic anatomy terms and stocking the house with tampons, Julia's budding womanhood was some other woman's job to lose sleep over. Jennifer would be dealing with it soon enough, she knew, sooner than seventeen, if she took some of the terrifying talk she'd overheard from the girls downstairs as any indication. They were ten going on twenty. Jennifer suddenly wondered if Julia was on the pill — she hadn't seen any packaging around. Surely she must know about the pill? Jennifer wondered if Cynthia knew about all of this? Probably. The girl must talk more about this stuff with her mother, right?

What if she didn't? And who was this J? Julia had never mentioned a boyfriend. Jennifer got up and went over to the dresser, looking at the photos tucked along the mirror frame, scanning the faces of all of the boys in the group shots, shocked at how much they looked like men. None seemed to be in more photos than the others.

Jennifer looked back at the note in her hand, folded it quickly and pushed it back into the pants pocket. She debated leaving them on the bed but instead dropped them on the floor, hoping they landed somewhere near their original resting place, although Jennifer couldn't imagine that anyone could tell that something was out of place in a sty like this.

The girls, deciding they had escaped any real trouble, had brought their conversation back to an audible level, and Jennifer was roused by the sound of laughter coming from the kitchen: "Oh, gross it's coming out your nose," someone shouted. She shook her head and followed it downstairs, put on a bright face and set about fixing them breakfast, then occupied herself for the rest of the morning ensuring their entertainment and transport home, but she couldn't put the note out of her mind.

When Tom and Ben came back in the door, she was sitting alone on the couch. Abby had beaten a glad retreat to her room, exhausted by a lack of sleep and the overwhelming energy of the others.

"Blessed quiet," Tom said, dropping onto the couch beside her. "How'd the party go?"

"I think the girls had fun. Well, at least the other two. That Emma is a little minx," Jennifer said tiredly. She had debated mentioning the note to Tom but had already decided against it, worried that he would overreact and do or say something stupid. He was somewhat overprotective of the girls. Besides, then she'd have to tell Julia she'd read the note, and that would not go over well. Surely Cynthia had seen fit to talk to the girl about this kind of thing; it wasn't Jennifer's place to interfere. She certainly wouldn't want Cynthia talking about this stuff with Abby. But it nagged at her.

Ben walked into the room on his way up to the shower, and Jennifer smiled at him. *Boys,* she thought, *are really just so much easier.* "How was practice?"

"Okay. Too early and I smell rank," he said, sitting down on her other side with a grin. "Wouldn't you agree?" he said, leaning forward for better effect.

"Oh, that is awful," she said, pushing him away but smiling. "Get into the shower immediately. Then come back here and Febreeze this couch. And Ben, DO NOT leave that equipment in the bag all week. Ugh."

He got up and was almost out of the room before Jennifer called after him. "Does Julia have a boyfriend?" He turned around.

"No," said Tom. "I mean she doesn't. Does she?"

Ben looked at them and shrugged. "I dunno." But he looked like he might.

Tom was still unconvinced. "No. She's too young for a boyfriend."

"She's seventeen, Tom."

"Talk to me when she's thirty, and maybe I'll allow it."

Jennifer rolled her eyes and turned her attention back to Ben.

"You haven't seen her hanging around with anyone? Maybe at school?" She tried to sound casual, but the fact that she was asking at all was so uncommon that it was hardly worth bothering.

Ben had seen his sister hanging around with someone. Hanging off of someone, actually. Julia hadn't made a big secret about dating Jesse Anderson — she practically had it tattooed to her forehead, but Ben had the sense that perhaps it wasn't news for parental ears. Unfortunately, he was not a master of the inside thought, so it was shared anyway.

"Jesse Anderson," Jennifer said. "Hmph. And what do you know about this Jesse Anderson, Ben?"

"Yes, Ben. What do you know about Jesse Anderson? What kind of name is Jesse? What is he, some kind of bandit?" Tom added most unhelpfully.

"All I know is that you didn't hear that name from me, because I would not like to be murdered in my sleep," Ben said, backing out of the room and running for the stairs.

"Well, we won't be seeing him again for the rest of the day," Tom said cheerfully in response to his wife's irritated look. "Why are you asking about Julia and dating, anyways? That's the last thing a brother would want to talk about. Not to mention a dad."

Jennifer knew then that she had been right in thinking that Tom would be a typical reactionary, unsympathetic father in these matters and the last person with whom she should be sharing her little discovery.

"I think Julia is having sex."

10

"A CTUALLY, I'M IMPRESSED, KID."
        Cynthia was sitting in her office with a
despondent Abby, holding a very professional and
not unkind rejection letter.

Dear Ms. Wilkes

Thank you for your recent submission to
our New Young Fiction issue. However, I
regret to inform it has not been selected for
our magazine.

Good luck in your future endeavors. And
keep writing.

Sincerely,
Marianne Holden
Fiction Editor
New City Magazine

"They didn't like it." Abby's voice floated up from the floor, where she had been lying despondently since she had come into the room, tossed the envelope at Cynthia, and declared that she was quitting writing.

"It doesn't say that anywhere," Cynthia replied, waving the letter over her.

"They didn't take it."

"Well, you can get used to that, kid. You should be thrilled they even used your name."

"You said it was good." Abby rolled over so that she could extend an accusatory finger. "*You* told me that it was good enough for public consumption!"

Cynthia eyed her young pupil and wondered briefly if the hormones of puberty were beginning to rear their ugly heads, or if writing just turned people into divas. She could rattle off at least a dozen conversations similar to this one that she'd had with grown writers whose work she had reviewed over the course of her career. People either infuriated that she hadn't like their books, or let down because she had and it hadn't resulted in any kind of monetary windfall.

"I did. And I meant it. But what I meant was that the story was done and it was time to move on to the next one. I hadn't intended to suggest that you should then send it off to a literary magazine and expect immediate publication," Cynthia said.

"Matt did it." The proof was right there on the wall, where hung a copy of one of his first published pieces. Cynthia had been so proud of him, so happy for him to have some evidence of the talent he was always questioning, always comparing to hers, that when the edition came out last year, she'd had the piece framed.

Abby's tone was thoroughly heartbroken. Cynthia was both exasperated and amused. All the eggshell-fragile egos, hers included, was why she'd jumped out of the arts arena years ago, choosing instead to discuss current affairs and share others' anecdotes of home life while she rested on the laurels of the words of her youth. "Not on his first story out the gate, honey, and please don't take this the wrong way, because you know I think you are a very promising writer, but he didn't do it at ten years old either."

"So I guess I should just wait until I'm older to even bother trying?" Abby was now stilling cross-legged, her face in her hands.

"Well, you could. If you just want to write to see your name somewhere. Or if you love writing like you say you do, maybe you just keep on writing for you."

Abby considered this. "I do like writing. Is that what you do? Just write for yourself?"

This was something that Cynthia hadn't done for a very long time. She could blame the kids, or the job — especially the job. There is a very real downside in trying to blend what you love with what you do to pay the rent. Compromises must be made, and you often end up doing such a bastardized version of what you had intended that you might as well be doing any other job. It can make you start to hate it.

It also sets you up to believe that doing what you love best is only valuable if it gets you something, and only if you can be the best at it. Why write if you aren't going to publish, why publish if you are not going to promote, why bother if all that work is just going to get panned or not sell, or not sell well enough?

But in the end the blame lay at her own feet. It was laziness, the fact that she'd chosen to cope with the emotional upheaval of her divorce by refusing to acknowledge her emotions and so hadn't since had a decent palette to help her create anything worthwhile. A fear that she would not be good any more, that maybe she never really had been.

So here she was, a poster child for a "not as I do" campaign, ragging on this kid for not recognizing the merits of art for art's sake. How sad.

"No, Abby, I don't. But I should. And in fact, I will if you will," Cynthia said, standing up and pulling Abby to her feet. "And while you're doing it, it doesn't mean you can't try to get your work out there for people to see. Just don't make that the goal, and you won't end up rolling on my floor every time you get some bad news. Because, believe me, if you want to be a professional writer, there is a lot of bad news coming your way."

She marched them both over to the writing desk, pulled some loose-leaf paper out of the drawer, and passed Abby a pencil.

"So let's get back on our horses, shall we. Write something."

"I don't know what to write about," Abby said, adding rather dramatically, "I'm uninspired."

"Oh, come on. Write about something that moves you, or concerns you, or makes you laugh. I don't care. Just put some words down there, and I'll try to do the same."

After a longish period of silence and a few more of lead scratching on paper, Cynthia looked up to discover their total output consisted of about a dozen words combined and an impressive collection of doodles.

"Okay. I guess we are both uninspired," she said, tossing her pencil across the room and leaning back in her chair. There was some energy that came from having your work out there, she had to admit it.

"You know, you could try submitting that story other places too, maybe shoot a little closer to home? Do you have a school paper or something?"

"Yes. But I'd never put it there."

"Why not, seems like a good place for it."

"Because I don't like getting laughed at. People think the school paper is lame."

"What people? Not the people who make the paper, I bet. It takes a lot of work to put out a paper. People wouldn't do it if they thought it was lame."

"Well, not all people. But my friends think it's lame. Emma says it's for retards," Abby said, dropping the volume as she finished, as unsure if "retards" was something you should say in front of adults, even if you were just quoting someone else.

"You shouldn't let your friends dictate what you do. Those aren't real friends," Cynthia said, surprised to hear Abby talking this way. She had seemed such an independent little thing when Cynthia first met her.

"Oh, brother," Abby said, dropping her pencil. "You know you say that and then other people tell you that you need to get along with people if you want to have friends. And then other people tell you that you should hang around with nice people but then they say that you should try to hang around with cool people. And then they say you are acting too old but then they call you baby and tell you to be mature and … you can't do all of those things at the same time, and it is really hard to keep all of it straight!" She pushed her chair away from the desk, dropping her arms helplessly to her sides.

Cynthia stared at her in surprise.

"Sorry. I didn't mean to yell. It's just really hard to try and figure this stuff out," Abby said.

Cynthia leaned forward, picked up the pencil Abby had dropped, and held it out to her. "Well, kiddo, why don't you write about that?"

//

C UPPING HIS HAND PROTECTIVELY AROUND THE FLAME, TOM
leaned forward to light the cigarette, drawing hard to
encourage enough tiny red embers to keep it going in
the strong fall wind. He wasn't supposed to be smoking, a
vice he'd purported to give up years ago, but one he couldn't
help indulging in when he was at the cottage. Something
about this place made him crave them deeply. Besides, he'd
had a rough go of it that day, so Jennifer had silently agreed
to turn a blind eye to it this time.

He caressed the lighter, polishing the pewter with a
slow rotation of his thumb. It was a smooth, solid weight in
the palm of his hand, like a stone from the river below. He
squeezed it as if resisting the urge to throw it into the water
at the end of the dock to watch it skim along the rhythmic
ripples melting into the bank.

That day he'd done what no father should ever have to
do — at least not the kind of father that Tom had been thus
far. He had sat Julia down in a chair at the cottage, and over

leftover pumpkin pie he had tried to talk to her about sex, and even more dangerously, about love.

Tom was the kind of father who did things, not said them. He showed up at events, even tried to show up on time. He brought gifts and paid for things and almost always said yes. He bore all the marks of a weekend, workaholic dad. He didn't try too hard be a role model; he was the first to admit he wasn't qualified. He tried very hard to make them happy, a million little apologies for whatever harm his actions might have caused them, and he generally kept a safe distance from the meaty parenting.

This discussion had certainly not been his idea. If he had his way, he would go back in time to the morning his wife told him that some punk kid was trying to stick it in his baby girl and just shoot himself before she started talking. Once he knew, however much as he didn't want to, there were some facts that even he understood must be faced. Someone was now going to have to ask some awkward questions. Was she having sex? Was she safe? Was she ready? Was this Jesse Anderson a decent punk at least? Where did he live, and where could Tom bury a body in case he wasn't decent?

Yet even at that point he was still under the blissful impression that his role in dealing with those questions was to make a quick call to Cynthia and see if she already had the situation in hand, and if not, to pass the buck quickly and never, ever, think about the topic again.

This sad delusion began to fade when Cynthia told him that while Julia had been to see a doctor and was pharmaceutically prepared for any sexual adventures she may be embarking on, Cynthia didn't know anything about a possible relationship and was unsure of Julia's emotional preparedness for such a situation. Cynthia had been thrown, and that threw Tom.

"Oh my god, she's having sex?" Cynthia had asked in a

strangled voice.

"Maybe."

"And what's this kid's name? Jesse? I have never even heard of this kid. Damn those cell phones. I'm burning them all. Those damn kids are going to have to start calling the damn house." The tirade was almost comical except for how hurt she sounded, how concerned. "I can't believe she didn't tell me this."

"She didn't tell anyone, Cyn. Jennifer found out by going through her pockets and then cornering Ben."

"Well ... good on Jennifer." Cynthia had to admit that while she was a great supporter of the idea that children needed their own space and respect, she was grateful that Tom's new wife had taken this moral low ground.

"So ... what do you think we should do?"

At this pivotal moment, Tom had presented a measured, eloquent case that this was really something that should be dealt with woman-to-woman but, to his surprise and horror, Cynthia had begged to differ.

"We are both going to have to talk to her about this, Tom. It can't just be me. She hates me right now."

"But I can't talk to her about ... this has got to be a mother's job," he argued, grasping at straws.

"Well, we've talked the mechanics out. I'm not a total idiot mother. But, Tom, you'll have to say something to her about it too. She seriously will not sit in a room with me these days. The minute I open my mouth she will decide this is either a criticism or parental authority run amok, and she will shut it down. Someone's going to have to make sure she's okay, and that's a father's job."

This he received with silence, trying desperately not to let the sense in what she was saying mingle in any way with his conscience.

"Come on, Tom, You won't need to say vagina or ovum or breasts or anything. You don't need to talk about the deed. Just tell her a little about respect and taking care of herself."

Easier said than done, Tom thought, hearing his ex-wife's impatient breathing on the other end of the line. She of all people must know that. He was a little taken aback that she would even suggest it. The adulterer giving the respect talk, she must be joking. Of all the crap and guilt and hurt feelings he had to drag around along with that title, surely he shouldn't have to carry this too.

"Well, maybe Jen could talk to her?" he suggested, wildly thinking he would shock her into taking control and seeing them all through another parental minefield.

"I am asking you to do this, Tom. *You*. She's our daughter and we have to deal with this, and I will do what I can, but I am asking you to step up here. It's not something I do often, so suck it up, would you?"

Over the years, when similar heavy issues had come up, Tom had been able to avoid really getting his hands dirty through his willingness to highlight his failings in this manner. He wasn't overly proud of himself for it, but it had proven highly effective. He'd even managed to avoid giving the sex talk to Matt … and he'd gladly do that a hundred times before he had to deal with "his *Jules*."

"Cynthia, can you hear yourself? Do you really think that I am the man be talking to her about that?" This time, however, it wasn't going to work.

"You're the dad here. You're the man she's got," Cynthia said, adding, "Trust me, I'd do it if I thought she'd listen."

She had never spoken like this to him before. He knew that she'd been having some issues with the kids. Matt staying at the house over the summer had been a first, and

Julia had been spending more time with them as well, but he had just chalked it up to general teenage rebellious ingrate syndrome. He didn't know that it had gotten so tense between Cynthia and the kids. She had never acknowledged that she couldn't handle it; one of her most striking, and alienating qualities was that Cynthia could handle anything. Once she said that, Tom knew his fate was sealed.

He had then fretted about it for over a week. What would he say? What would *she* say? How could he look at her and tell her how important it was to look for somebody who would put your interests first, and talk to you and listen to you and only want what's best for you, without offering himself up for her criticism, her disdain.

Jennifer had proven really wonderful during this time, offering suggestions and advice, easing his nerves and defending his choices, defending him. "We've been married for eleven years, Tom. The only other woman you've ever been with is her mother. You do not need to apologize to anyone for your life, not any more. You made a mistake, maybe, in how you handled things, but you're hardly a womanizer or a deadbeat. I know it, Cynthia must know it too, or she wouldn't have asked you to do this. Have a little faith that Julia knows it too."

He didn't know what Julia knew, or what she thought about much of anything except popular rock bands and the cost of teenage living. It seemed that was all they had been talking about for as long as he could remember. For all the love he had for her, he didn't really know her, certainly didn't know what she thought about him. What any of them thought.

The idea that your kids can just one day start to see themselves as separate from you, start living lives you don't control and begin to see and judge you as people, was something Tom found more terrifying than bringing them home in the first place.

He took another slow, satisfying drag and looked back over his shoulder through the window, where Julia and Jennifer were talking animatedly. He was amazed that he was looking at two women and how he hadn't noticed that before. Tom couldn't say when that transformation had occurred, when his Jules had become a woman. He closed his eyes, trying to recall when exactly she had grown into her big blue eyes and stringbean limbs and evolved into this beautiful creature, someone that men would want. How could that be?

He did remember many things about her. For all that he missed not being with her every day, he did remember that she loved sunflowers best and that she was never afraid to hook a worm, not even the first time. He knew that she had a tiny mole at the back of her knee, that her blood type was B+, the same as his. Oh god, and he remembered the time he spent in a hospital bed, needle strapped to his arm so they could use some of it as they prepared her for surgery that time the car had rolled. How Cynthia had sounded when she called him, so frantic and blaming herself for the bad turn, one of the few other times she had ever shown herself to be vulnerable, holding his hand, knowing that he was the only one that could do anything for her and that all there was for her was to wait, worried they might lose her. But they hadn't. They had carried her safely to this point where he could now sit and talk to her like an adult.

Because instead of the awkward, angry confrontation he'd been expecting once he started "the talk," what they'd had instead had been an awkward and sort of amusing back-and-forth that left them both mildly embarrassed but unscathed. He did have Cynthia to thank for some of that he knew. Despite her claims that it would be disastrous, she had felt required to broach the topic of dating with Julia before she headed to her dad's for Thanksgiving, and in a class move, she'd taken the heat when Julia called foul and accused her of spying when Jesse's name came up, more to save Ben than Jennifer, Tom guessed. Cynthia hadn't gotten far, but managed to discover that Julia and Jesse were not making the beast with two backs — though the only reason given was that apparently Jesse was a "dill weed."

When he sat her down that morning, Julia had been suspicious but not unprepared for the fumbling advice. She'd cut him off shortly after he began his "Julia you are woman now" speech.

"Dad, no. Listen, I don't know what Mom told you, but I am not doing … anything."

"Oh. Oh, good. I mean fine, I mean you should do what you want to do … or not do anything. I mean, you shouldn't do what you don't want to do. That's for sure."

"Umm, okay. Sounds good. Will do." She'd stood up to leave and he almost let her before he grabbed her hand.

"I mean you are a special girl … a special woman. And you should never let anyone make you feel any different."

Blushing, she wouldn't look right at him, but she didn't move.

"I know. Okay."

"And you are so smart and so talented, even when you try not to be, it's like you can't even help it, and you need someone who can see that and who will only respect you for it."

"Okay."

"Because it takes a very strong man to be good enough for a strong woman, you know. It's harder for a lot of them to live up to that than even they may realize."

She'd looked at him pointedly, and he felt his face getting hot. As much as he wanted to turn his eyes away from her then, he kept them focused, offering as much an apology as an explanation. She remained silent, giving him the smallest hint of a nod, as much a sign of acceptance as understanding.

"And you can tell me anything," he continued after a moment. "Jennifer too," he added, knowing she was pretending not to listen from the living room. "You should tell us anything you want to."

"Okay."

"Because we only want what's best for you, you know that?"

"I know."

"And your mom wants that too. You know that, right?"

"Yeah."

"I mean, there is nothing in the world that she would not do for you, you do know that, right?"

"Gawd. Yes. I get it. I know."

"I love you, Jules, you know that too, right?"

"Yeah. Yes, I know."

She didn't say it back, but that she'd squeezed his hand when he said it was more genuine affection expressed between them than had happened in forever. He found himself staring at his daughter through tear-washed eyes.

"Jeez. Dad, don't start crying, this is, like embarrassing enough," she said with a bit of a grin, releasing his hand and thumping his arm. "You're getting soft in your old age." Having saved the moment from spiralling into Hallmark territory, she walked out of the room, stating, "I'm going to go pack."

And Tom had headed out to the dock to get a little air and take some time before he'd have to rehash with Jennifer, and to let the wind dry the salt water threatening to leak out the corners of his eyes.

Lost in his own thoughts, he watched the light sparkling on the water and remained there until he heard the car horn calling his kids back to their mother. He watched them exit the cottage and load their stuff in the trunk, Ben hollering "Dibs" before offering a quick wave and folding his ever-growing frame in beside his mother. Julia opened her door then looked at him before blowing him a kiss, saying "Thanks, Dad," and getting in behind them. He drank it in like warm honey, the feeling enhanced by the slight, approving nod Cynthia gave him from the drivers' seat. He was struck by the shared mannerisms of mother and daughter. Tom watched the car back up the drive as Cynthia ferried them to her parents' place for yet another turkey dinner.

He watched until he could no longer see the car lights amongst the trees or hear the hum of the engine. Until there was nothing to see but the tracks she'd left on the dirt country road. When Jennifer came out to join him, telling him that Abby was sleeping in front of the fireplace, and reached for his hand, making no comment about the smoking, he could not remember a time when he had been so damn proud of them all.

He knew in that moment that he was truly and blissfully happy. It had been years since he'd let himself feel that way, like he had the right to be so content, that he had earned it. When you've done the worst thing that you can do to someone else, when you've signed on for the role of the uncontested bad guy, it seems impossible that you can ever reclaim the right to create a new life as good as the one you'd ruined.

But maybe it was time to be happy. He wasn't getting any younger, and it wasn't like you got a chance to come back and do it all over again, you can only take a look at where you are currently standing and decide whether or not you are going to let your life be good or not. It didn't matter if you thought you deserved it, or if you were entitled to it, all that mattered was that you decided to opt out of being unhappy when you had the chance.

Tom looked down at the lighter in his hand for a moment before a quick flick of the wrist sent it dancing lightly over the waves for a second then disappearing from view. He slid his now unencumbered hand around his wife's waist and strolled with her up the dock.

"I think it's time I gave up that crap for good."

12

IN THE SUMMER CYNTHIA READ THE CANADIAN AUTHORS. It was then, in that time of pure breezes, warm winds, and dragonflies, that she could bear the frozen tundras, broken fields, and farmers, and those rain-soaked victims of incest. Nestled in a wooden chair, a sandal hooked on a porch beam, she could muster up the fortitude to survive those ill-fated and desperate journeys towards intimacy and forgiveness. Blessed with a few weeks of the kind of summer heat that allows for reading atop a water float, and she might even tackle the Russians. You couldn't read those kinds of books in the winter months, not when the Toronto days started too late and ended too early and everything was grey and cold. Reading those books then was hard work and made her tired. More often than not she would end up asleep on the couch after a few pages, the book slipping to the floor with a thud.

In the winter Cynthia read cookbooks, but then those cold, dark months had always been about survival. She went for the really sumptuous kind that featured lavish colour photos of confident, photogenic cooks preparing equally appealing meals. These were books she could fall into and feel satisfied, nourished. A few years earlier, when her collection of these gorgeous tomes grew a little too big for a woman whose culinary legend was built on her impressive recall of take-out restaurant phone numbers, she had subscribed to a "lifestyle" magazine that offered the same feeling in a less permanent package. She was also a fan of the free magazines at the liquor store, keeping an eye out for the newest edition whenever she was picking up a bottle of wine for dinner. On days when the kids were out and she had forgone a proper meal for the convenience of tinned soup heated up in the microwave, Cynthia would curl up on the couch with one of these on her lap, a glass of wine by her side, and she'd dive into the recipes, imagining the menus of elegant dinner parties she never intended to throw.

But the fall was a twilight time, when her tastes were erratic and she was most open to a new author or genre. This year especially, she felt herself more willing to explore, more desperate to sink herself into a blanket of words.

She had hardly returned to work when she had been overcome with the desperate need to hole up with a stack of novels and a comfortable chair. Ignoring the fact that her decision seemed textbook of some sort of middle-aged breakdown, she had requested and been rather grudgingly granted permission to use a week of her large stash of vacation time, and she had made her way back to her parents' cottage. Since Thanksgiving she had been feeling antsy, uncomfortable, and listless — all the things she tended to feel before the onset of a creative burst. And because it had been so long since she had experienced one, she wanted to do everything in her power to foster it. The goodwill that seemed to be knitting itself between she and Tom, thanks to Abby, made it easier for her to say goodbye to the kids and take this time just for herself.

At the end of a six-hour journey, made pleasant by the music playlist her kids had put together for her (a gesture spurred by both the freedom her absence might afford them, and some concern with the exhibition of even more unpredictable behaviour on the part of their primary caregiver), Cynthia had felt unnaturally energized as she stepped out into the brisk pre-winter air. Getting her suitcase and initial supplies down the rickety steps to the cottage had taken a single trip, but the books required two more that had dulled to some extent the spring in her step and left her remembering why it was she should use the treadmill she'd bought several years ago and promptly stored in the basement.

She had considered avoiding this hassle and simply bringing the new reading gadget she'd received as a gift from the kids, but only briefly and only because Ben had whined as he'd helped her pack the car about why she was refusing to move out of the dark ages. To him it was unthinkable that you'd carry around all these dusty pages when you could stuff all the reading material you'd ever want to see into something you could shove in a coat pocket. But she'd never really gotten the hang of ordering the books. How do you choose when your library consists of what seems like all the books in the universe? And she couldn't break the habit of licking her index finger before "turning" the pages, leaving little slimy trails across the screen. She knew she couldn't explain (and also that she didn't have to), but there's just something about a book.

She had selected a large collection of hardcovers when she stopped by the library on her way out of town. She always preferred the feel of a hardcover in her hands, and since she was counting on her time at the lake to be a constant reading binge, she'd needed a heavy load. When uninterrupted by petty annoyances such as the dietary and entertainment needs of her brood, or a horrifically complicated plot, Cynthia could easily whip through a book a day.

Her choices consisted of novels ranging from guilty pleasure chick lit, to thrillers for exhilarating midnight reading, to a few heavy-hitting classics she was determined to try to get through this time ... her third attempt at *Ulysses*. She had added to these a couple of science fiction books she'd picked up based solely on their brightly-hued covers and a few of the random volumes she'd received as review copies over the years but never bothered with.

All of these she had dumped on the porch her parents had glassed in when they'd decided to retire here, before realizing how isolating the winters would be and hightailing to Florida with the other snowbirds. It was Cynthia's favourite place to read.

She piled the books into piles beside the mesh lounge chair she favoured for longer stints, and had made the first cursory tour of the cabin looking for telltale signs of animal invasion before she had expended the rest of her initial energy. She felt she'd earned the right to a cup of tea and a moment to contemplate the collection of reading material she had amassed, and how she would go about tackling it.

At home she could only read one book at a time, when she had the time, which wasn't often. With all the words she had to deal with during the workday, she found herself too exhausted to think about diving into any more. Plus there were the kids and the commitments and the rapidly growing number of ridiculous television shows that could suck you in, even though they offered absolutely nothing of value and often very little in the way of entertainment.

Here she would gorge on printed pages. This was the place that she'd learned to read, learned to love spending hot summer days sprawled out on the floor, a bowl of grapes by her side and filling her head with all it could hold, evenings passing by in a blur under the covers with a flashlight. Not much had changed save for some winterizing and the installation of electricity, which had tipped her reading habit into a full-blown addiction. This was a place of late mornings and late nights, a place with no schedules, or Internet, or telephone — a place where all there was to do was eat, swim, and rest, and read and write. Here she could easily flip between stories like her kids flipped television channels. She could stay up until five in the morning completely absorbed. Or at least there had been a time when she could. She was hoping she could get it back on this trip; in fact, she was counting on it.

It was just a matter of where to begin. Looking around as she sipped from her steaming cup, Cynthia momentarily forgot the new glossy "town" books at her feet and wandered over to the old pine bookcase and its selection of yellowed and well-thumbed paperbacks from past summers. She scanned the collection of *Reader's Digest* short story anthologies and the set of 1960s-era Funk and Wagnall encyclopedias, books that her parents had collected and she would not let them get rid of. She had made her first mark as a writer on the inside covers of those books, before she could even spell, waves of ink she'd sent rolling across the pages, leaving no blank space unfilled. She'd been spanked for that, she remembered, but it had been worth it.

She let her hands glide gently across the volumes. Her mother's bodice-ripper romances, the Hardy Boys books that had tricked Ben into becoming a reader, the requisite collection of Anne books — a staple of any young girl's library. She pulled *Rilla of Ingleside* from the shelf knowing that it would most certainly be read while she was there.

She always ended up with her nose stuck in these old, moldy books, regardless of how many fresh best-selling fiction titles she armed herself with. The books that you loved when you were a child, that made you love reading, stick with you. This was her time, and she could read what she liked.

Once she had plucked her old standbys, she went to fetch a notepad and pen from her purse. Even as an adult the routines of cottage life have to be observed. As a young girl, Cynthia had always kept track of the books she read over the summer. At first she did it mostly to show that she had read more books than her older sister, but had since come to find a great sense of accomplishment in finishing a book on the list. Especially with challenging ones, which suddenly made her think of Abby. It was funny to recall that before she'd been old enough to get an adult library card of her own, she had begged her mother to take out books on her behalf.

By the time she was in her teens, the lists had become her trophies, proof of how much she had accomplished, and as an adult they morphed into a treasure map of her own making. She would spend happy hours scanning the dust jackets and flipping the books open to random pages to test out the language. More than plot or characters, it was the words themselves that Cynthia loved. The flow, the pacing, and the way they looked as they spilled across the page.

To Cynthia, creating a reading list required all of the delicacy of making a mixed tape. She didn't want to careen from a no-brainer into a heavy plotted saga with a character key on the front page. And while she liked reading on a common theme, she certainly didn't want to read two really depressing books in a row — that could ruin you. She returned to the porch and sat chewing absently on a pen cap, jotting down the names, scratching them out and moving them around until she was satisfied.

Then she looked out the window at the water, not yet frozen in the river, though the weather had most definitely turned. It wouldn't be long before you'd be able to walk out there. Fear of sounding like some naturalist head case aside, Cynthia felt like it was the river that had first called to her when she'd been up the month before, and she hadn't been able to stop thinking about the place since. It was more than the river, of course, it was the ghosts that lived along its banks; the memories of she and her sister, her parents, mostly of Tom and the kids. These were always with her, but this year she seemed to have stirred them from their tranquil resting spot at the back of her mind. She had been finding them around every corner.

Even after the divorce, Cynthia and Tom had often come to the island at the same time, working around the kids' school breaks, trying to make the back and forth of holidays as easy as possible on them, and of course both their parents were here. But they had, up until this past Thanksgiving, managed to run miraculously independent lives while staying in such close proximately. At some point after the break-up, the whole village seemed to join forces and, aware when they were all present, they did a marvellous job of running gentle interference to avoid having any of the adults bumping into each other unexpectedly and causing some undefined but genuinely concerning scene.

This year had been different. Abby had spied Cynthia at the supermarket within hours of her arrival, and instead of stepping unseen into the next aisle to linger around the cereals until she'd finished paying, the girl had run giddily up to see her, excited the way children often are to find someone they know from one place turn up, as if by magic, in another.

Unable to ignore her, Cynthia had been led into a public conversation with Jennifer about when and how to get the kids from one place to another, as locals waited to see what kind of fireworks would surely ensue. But nothing happened. It had been so civil and unexciting that the talk in the coffee shop later that afternoon was likely how they had placed their time and care into such careful acts of avoidance and subterfuge for nothing.

After this, the idea of blocking out her awareness of Tom's presence there seemed a ridiculous waste to her as well, so Cynthia had stopped. And in little bits, since she'd left, the memories of him, of them together on that island, had been coming back. She found that as much as they had once hurt to think about, not that long ago, she had missed them. She felt it might be time to let that part of her back into her life, so she'd come back to visit with the ghosts of her past to see how they treated her now. Cynthia looked down at her hands to see that she was already writing.

13

The Island King

"IT'S NOT THAT COLD," HE'D SAY THROUGH PALE BLUE LIPS.
The water was never cold as far as he was concerned.
The bugs never bit you, and the bears never tore up
the garbage, and the outhouse never smelled either. Not
on his island.

It was my island too. I could climb just as many rocks and
catch just as many fish as he could, even if I was a girl. I was
just as good at pumping the well water without muddying
up my feet. I was even better than he was at toasting up
marshmallows without singeing them. Mine were always
perfectly golden and melt-in-your-mouth delicious. I was
known for it. A legend.

But I always knew the water was cold enough to steal
the scream right out of your throat if you jumped straight
off the dock like a lunatic. And I knew the 'skito bites could
keep you up all night long, half crazy with their itching,
but even that was preferable to the deerflies always angling
to rip a whole chunk out of an unprotected shoulder or

the unguarded big toe poking out of the sand as you lay helplessly buried to the neck under a mound of earth packed so tight, your arms felt encased in cement.

He, however, was the self-crowned king of the island. He knew every gully and every tree like the back of his hand. He could ferret out the juiciest wild strawberries and knew how to suck the most flavour out of a winterberry leaf, rolling it tight as a Cuban cigar and jamming it into the hollow between cheek and gums like ballplayer's chewing tobacco.

In the summer he could somehow reject his Celtic DNA, turning a deep honey gold from head to shirtless torso to his shoeless feet. He'd have gone pantless if he thought they'd let him get away with it.

Me, I'd burn — every summer fast and furious. I'd arrive pale as the crescent moon and by the end of day one would be suffering the effects of a raging sunburn that required, without fail, that I spend the first of my precious weeks penned in and covered in cold cream doing the same puzzles with the same infuriating missing pieces on the porch, watching the world go by.

My only solace then was his drive-by water gun showers and the occasional presentation of an "authentic" Indian arrowhead dug up from somewhere deep in the mysterious woods that surrounded our cabins and made us feel like we were living on the edge of the world.

When I was finally free, he'd make amends for his near total abandonment, sitting with me on the waterlogged dock telling me alternating stories of his great adventures and of how bored he'd been without me as he gently picked the tempting flakes of peeling skin off the places that I couldn't reach.

I loved it when he did that; his hand absently brushing against my neck, along my back to where the brightly coloured nylon of my bathing suit pressed against my shoulder blades, occasionally snapping the straps, but not meanly; I wasn't burnt by then. It felt cozy and friendly when we sat like this, the two of us sharing our secrets in the sun. It felt happy and easy and fun.

Until the summer that it didn't. That summer I arrived to find him bigger than I remembered, bigger than I could ever imagine him being. That was the summer my mother made me wear a cotton harness under my shirts. Even when it was scorching hot and I was just sitting on the dock, my nose buried in a Nancy Drew book, waiting for him to finish playing his stupid war tag with the other stupid boys who said I wasn't good enough to play.

The same summer he'd stolen a cigarette from his dad's pack for us to try hidden away in the woods. We'd held the ashes in our palms, terrified we'd start a forest fire. It was the summer our mothers wouldn't let us go on our annual sleepover on the teeny little sand bar offshore, where we'd been holing up in a pup tent since as long as we could remember, telling corny ghost stories so that we'd get scared, but not too scared.

That summer I burned again, even worse than before in the two-piece bathing suit my mother had bought me so that I wouldn't get "tan lines," something that concerned her greatly. He still came to see me trapped in my mesh prison, driving by on the cruiser bike he'd bought himself over the winter with the money he'd made stocking shelves at his dad's grocery store.

When I made it back outside, he sat with me on the dock, inspecting my war wounds and talking up a storm. He put his hand on my neck, but it was heavier that summer, and clammy. When it slid from my neck to my shoulder, I felt the weight of his whole arm, his muscles flexing just underneath that golden skin. It seemed as solid as the dead heads floating by below.

I felt his leg pressed beside mine close, but uncomfortable. His thigh now covered in a dusting of dark hairs, and mine smooth as silk. I could smell him too, but it was no longer the safe smell of pine gum, sunscreen and sweat, but a mix of musk and cigarettes. We shared no secrets; we didn't say anything after a while. All I could hear was his breathing, and that was how I knew he was leaning nearer, even though I had my eyes squeezed so tight that all I could see was the electric storm playing against my eyelids. And I wanted so badly to get away that I was willing to risk freezing to death in that cold black water just to be able to slip down into that deep, safe darkness.

But I didn't want him to let go.

14

DEAR MS. WILKES.

Thank you for you submission to our New Young Fiction issue. We are delighted to inform you that we very much enjoyed your short story and are proud to have it as part of our upcoming issue. Please see the attached contract and suggested revision sheet and we will be in touch.

We look forward to working with you.

Sincerely,
Marianne Holden
Fiction Editor
New City Magazine

15

"WHY THE HELL DID YOU SHOW IT TO HER?" ELLEN asked, sitting in Cynthia's festively decorated living room, the story in one hand, a glass of wine in the other. And it wasn't even noon.

"What do you mean? She asked to see what I was working on. How could I know she'd take it?"

Cynthia was hung over, clad in a fuzzy robe covered in snowmen and pacing through the debris of discarded wrapping paper left over from the previous day's gift exchange free-for-all. She kicked a ball of it into the fireplace, remembering how happy she had been only hours ago.

Matt, so missed at Thanksgiving, had come home accompanied by a lovely young woman for whom he seemed absolutely head over heels, a girl nowhere near as vapidly timid and overly sexualized as the ones he had dated before. Julia, having received a new computer, as well as a letter of early acceptance to her first choice school in Nova Scotia earlier in the week, was being positively civil … even to Matt's girl.

And in what Cynthia thought was a sign of immense maturity on everybody's part, she had agreed to having a mid-day Christmas brunch with the kids at Tom's house before heading to her usual solo Christmas Day Matinee.

"I just mean, what were you thinking showing THAT story to her?" Ellen said again, trying to be gentle but seemingly finding the words difficult to get out over the giant I Told You So sitting at the back of her throat.

"I don't know. I don't know. I didn't even think about it," Cynthia said, perching momentarily on the edge of a chair before getting up and pacing some more. "I just can't believe this happened."

They had all made it to Tom's, and with the help of some champagne, they also made it through the luncheon and were just finishing off dessert, planning their various exits, lulled into a false sense that this was actually going to work out all right, when it happened.

"I was so happy to hear you got your letter this week, Julia," Jennifer said again, trying to fill up the final moments of requisite dinner chat. "It's nice to hear we have two intellectuals in the family."

"Well, not just two," Tom said quickly, "don't forget Abby." He looked fondly at the little girl who seemed so thrilled to have them all sitting together in one room.

"Oh, nice. Thanks, all," said Ben from the corner, over top of the video game he was playing."

"All of my children are talented," Cynthia said quickly, jumping to Ben's defence.

"Oh, yeah, what's Ben's talent?" Matt asked.

"Don't you remember, Matt, Ben walks on water," Julia replied. It was no secret that Ben was the parental favourite. But then everybody loved Ben.

"Oh, stop it," Cynthia said. "But yes, Jules, we are all

thrilled that you got into the school you wanted, honey. It's great." She then lifted her glass and drained it, deciding to go while the going was good and while they all seemed to be getting along, but Jennifer continued.

"And not just school to celebrate, huh?" Jennifer said, giving Julia a little wink. Her cheeks were flushed and she was giggling. She didn't normally drink, and she had been acting a little silly.

Cynthia perked up, wondering what new piece of Julia's life she'd been shut out of and trying, unsuccessfully, not to resent the fact that Jennifer might be in the know, but looking at her daughter, she noted confusion on her face.

"What do you mean?" Julia asked her stepmother.

"Oh, you know, Jules. The story. The letter," Jennifer said.

"What are talking about, Jennifer?" Julia asked, looking somewhat relieved and making a slight tipping gesture with her hand to indicate that maybe Jennifer had had enough.

"The letter, from the magazine, the story," Jennifer said. "Don't be mad, Jules, I saw it in Abby's room. You know, she's always peeking at your stuff. Don't be mad, honey, it was so good. You shouldn't be embarrassed, that's a great magazine. I've seen copies in the doctor's office." Jennifer nodded sagely to Cynthia.

"Jennifer, I don't know what you are talking about," Julia said, confused. "I haven't been writing any stories."

"Oh, go get it, Abby honey, your sister's being shy," Jennifer said, waving her arm at Abigail with one hand and reaching for her glass with the other, a satisfied smile on her face. "Don't shine a light in a bushel ... that's what I always say."

The boys tossed each other a look and snorted, but Abby sat frozen in her seat, staring at the floor, and all of a sudden Cynthia started to feel a bit uneasy.

"Go on," Jennifer encouraged her daughter, giving her a little shove. "I'm sure Cynthia here would like to read it. Have you read it, Cynthia? You're the expert, you must know it's good." Then, seeing Cynthia's face she added, "Oops. Sorry. Well, Jules it's going to be published anyway, no reason to be shy. Look, Abs, Julia's not mad, hop on up there like a good bunny, you're keeping everybody in suspense."

Julia looked bewildered as Abby slowly slid off her chair and headed for the stairs. After a few moments, when the silence in the room became uncomfortable and she hadn't come back down, Jennifer sent Tom up after her. Cynthia tried to make a move to quell the bad, indefinable feeling rising in her chest, but Jennifer just filled their glasses and hollered up the stairs after them.

Tom came back down just as Cynthia was chugging the last out of her glass. He was staring at her and holding a few sheets of paper in his hands. "Did you write this?" he asked her.

"Of course she did. Who else would've," Jennifer said, elbowing her stepdaughter. "Take a bow, kiddo, s'really good. Young love. Nice. Guess you made up with that Jesse."

Tom held the sheets out to Cynthia. She saw the words "The Island King" written across the top of the page and thought she might be sick.

"Did you write this?" he asked again.

"Yes," she whispered, taking the papers as everyone else at the table looked around uncomfortably.

"What is going on?" Julia asked. Matt looked quickly from his mother to his father to the shifting look on Jennifer's face and nodded once. In unison, the kids all stood up and beat it into the other room.

"What *is* going on?" Jennifer asked, setting down her glass and eyeing them both.

"Abby submitted this story to the magazine," Tom said, turning his focus away from Cynthia for a moment. "But Cynthia wrote it."

"*You* wrote this," Jennifer said, lunging forward and grabbing the sheets from Cynthia's hand, eyes skimming the page again before she threw them on the ground.

"Jen," Tom started, but she threw her hand up, cutting him off.

"*You* wrote this? And gave it to *my* kid." Her voice was rising with every word.

"I didn't give it to her, she must have seen it at my office," Cynthia said, then turning to Tom, "Are you telling me she submitted this? As her own work?" Tom nodded.

"You get out. You get the hell out of my house. Stay the hell away from my kid and you stay the hell away from my husband," Jennifer was roaring now, and Tom reached out to try and steady her, but she slapped him away. He pushed his hands through his hair and said nothing.

Cynthia got to her feet too, embarrassed that they'd seen this, that Tom had read it. She was more than embarrassed. She was enraged.

"Are you fucking kidding me, lady?" She was not going to be talked to like this, not by that woman. No damn way. "You go ahead and keep that little klepto away from me if you can. I never asked her to start hanging around, I certainly never asked for her to take my things and masquerade them as her own, though you must be pretty proud, like mother and all that."

"Cynthia!" Tom shouted, only to be once again waved aside.

"And as for your husband here, if I'd wanted Tom I'd have him. Don't you ever forget that he begged me to let him stay. If it wasn't for that kid up there, you wouldn't even be a memory."

"Jesus, Mom, that's enough. All of you, that's enough." They all turned and saw Matt standing the doorway, his arms around Abby, who was choking back tears.

"I'm sorry. I'm sorry, Cynthia. I'm sorry, Mommy. But I told the kids at school I was good. I just wanted to show them. I know it was bad. I didn't mean ... I'm sorry for everything. I just wanted people to think I was good. I'm sorry. Please."

Her face was so pale, so frightened, so young.

"Ah, shit," Cynthia said under her breath, feeling like the worst person in the world. "Honey, I didn't mean what I said, I was just...."

"Don't you talk to her, don't you say another word to her. You get out of here. Come here baby, come to Mommy, it's okay." Jennifer threw out her arms and grasped for her daughter, but Abby just pushed further into Matt's legs. "I said c'mere," her mother snapped.

Tom just stared at Abby and didn't say anything.

"You all need to grow the hell up," Matt said quietly, hoisting Abby up in his arms and heading for the hallway. Cynthia could see the stone-faced look on Julia's face, Ben's winkled forehead, a classic sign that he was upset, and the look of intense discomfort on Britney, who was trying desperately to disappear into the wall. They all had their coats on.

"Where are you going?" Jennifer called out after him.

"We need to get out of here, and Gramma's at Aunt Jayne's and expecting us for dinner." Then Matt slammed the door behind them and Jennifer burst into sobs.

As she did this, Cynthia bent quickly to pick up the sheets and headed for the door as she watched Tom pivot between the two of them, trying to decide which discussion he wanted to have the least. She knew that was one decision she was happy to make for him and ran for it, realizing when she hit the street that she was too drunk to drive home. She hailed a cab, gave the driver her address and then a hefty tip when they arrived, as if this form of Christmas charity could fix any of the ugliness she'd just been party to.

She fell into bed and a bottle of wine and hadn't moved until Ellen knocked on her door expecting their annual "Kids at Their Father's Boxing Day Brunch."

"Well. I'm sorry, Cyn. I'm really sorry for what happened. And I am truly, honestly sorry for having to say this, but I told you not to get messed up in this stuff. There are very good reasons why exes stay exes."

Cynthia looked at Ellen, disgusted, and threw herself on the couch, holding a pillow over her face. "I am not in love with Tom, Ellen. Do you hear me? I am *not* in love with Tom. I do not want to be with Tom," she yelled through the foam.

"I hear what you are saying, yes. It does beg the question though, Cyn, why are you writing love stories about Tom, don't you think? And why you are showing those stories to his kid?"

"It's not a love story."

"Bullshit."

"Well, it's not a story about Tom. I mean, obviously it is, but not really, it's … it's fiction, for god's sake. And as for sharing it, we were writing together. She wanted to see what I was working on. So I showed her."

"She's not a critic, she's a ten-year-old girl, Cyn."

"There's nothing dirty in it."

"It's about you and her dad."

"Well, I certainly didn't expect her to give it to her mother, if that's what you are implying. Or to plagiarize it and send it out to get it published in a frigging magazine."

Cynthia felt a sick little flicker of pride as she said this. Her anger over having the piece shared without her knowledge had been tempered somewhat by the fact that the piece had been accepted, and by *New City* too. Even that cow Jennifer, who could read, it turned out, had liked it. Cynthia still had it. It was the only bright spot in the whole damn mess.

"God, Ellen, you sound just like her. As If I'm the man stealer, as if I'm the one who is trying to bust up the family. Her kid comes sniffing around my house and I welcome her in, and I swallow my pride and let that woman host *my* family for Christmas dinner so her kid can have some fantasy get-together, and I am the asshole?"

"Trust me. I do not have one positive thing to say about Tom or Barbie, and you know it. This isn't about them. It is about you, and what I am saying to you is you gave a little kid a grown-up story that outlined in detail how you and her father are soulmates, and then as far as I can tell played the wounded party when word got out and took a little kid to task for it … and spewed out some pretty nasty shit while you were at it." Ellen took a swig from her glass.

Cynthia heard this, even through the fog of the wine and the hurt feelings and the excuses she was carrying around by the bucketful. The memory of Abby's face surfaced, and Cynthia could almost feel how devastated and confused the kid must have been about what Cynthia had said about her, and about her mother. The one thing she'd promised Jennifer she would not do when she took Abby on she had done, at full volume, in front of the whole family. At Christmas.

"I *am* the asshole," she moaned and dropped her head into her lap, covering it with her arms and rocking slowly back and forth.

What had she been thinking making this little kid a confidante? Expecting her to act like the grown up she was pretending to be. Working through her own life issues with a child. Hadn't she learned anything from the mistakes she'd made with Julia? When the hell was she ever going to learn?

"I never meant for this to happen. And she obviously never meant to pass it on to her mom. I don't even think she knew what it was about. Not really," Cynthia said, feeling the guilt spreading through her like a hot liquid metal. She could practically taste it.

"Oh, god the things I said about her ... and she was standing right there." It was all coming back, the shame on Abby's face, the reproach on Matt's. Oh, and that poor girlfriend of his trapped there too. He'd brought her home to meet the family, and his mother caused a domestic that torpedoed Christmas. He would never forgive her. She bet none of them would. She didn't even know where they all were now.

"The kids are never going to speak to me again."

Ellen came to sit beside her and patted her back. Now that her point had been made, she was happy to play the role of comforter. "Of course they will, honey. If only so they can come back and claim this bounty," she said, gesturing at the bags and boxes still tucked under the tree.

"Don't joke," Cynthia said from under her arms. But she laughed a little.

"Oh, I don't think there's much else to do at the moment." After scanning the pages in her hand again, Ellen added, "The story is good, you know."

"Thanks."

"I'm happy to see that you're writing again."

"Yeah."

"But, just a suggestion from a humble music geek, but maybe you need to stop thinking about the past so much and focus a little on the here and now? I'm just saying that may be a bit of a safer approach."

Cynthia rolled herself around so that her head was now resting Ellen's lap. "Oh, it'd be safer all right. Aging, single, mother of three, past her prime sits in an overpriced home feeling sorry for herself because she has no life. Scintillating stuff."

"Well, don't forget the charming, quirky sidekick best friend and voice of wisdom."

"Of course not ... Ellie, I hear what you are saying, and maybe I am playing with fire here, but you have to understand, it's not that I want him back. I know that's never going to happen. We aren't even the same people now. Watching him with Abby, I can even see that he's better with Jennifer, she lets him call the shots, and I never did. I know if we went back there that we still wouldn't have worked out. I just don't want to forget what if felt like when I didn't know that. You know what I mean?"

"Listen, Cyn. I get that you loved him, and I know he loved you too."

Cynthia looked up at her sadly. "Do you know, sometimes it actually feels like that never happened. Like we were never right. But there was a really long time when we were everything to each other, and now it's like I even doubt I could have felt like that about Tom, or about anybody. I honestly don't think I could now, and that's not terrible, I know. But I think I am just sorry I spent so long ignoring that. I doubt that the kids could even imagine that we had ever been that happy together. I don't think Ben even remembers a time when we were a family. That just breaks my heart, El."

Cynthia was crying now and sat up to grab a tissue from the coffee table. "Therapy is bad for the sinuses."

"Listen to me now. You have done a great job making a life for those kids, and don't you ever apologize for that. Whatever you think you may or may not have done right, I don't ever want to hear you say you didn't do all you could for those kids."

"Including traumatizing them on Jesus's birthday?"

"Oh, I'm not saying you didn't mess them up some, honey. But I think that's a membership requirement to the parents club. I'm not speaking as an official authority here, as you well know, though I take a damn amount of pride in the role I've played with those kids myself. But I am telling you that you have not done more than your average parent does to screw up their kids. And they love you, Cyn, underneath it all, you must know they love you. You are a good mom, and you did a good job, so you can stop worrying. Plus, kids are resilient out of necessity and design. Trust me, they will all bounce back from this, even the little girl. And you'll be here when they come around, so in the meantime, maybe you can take a little bit of time to get your head screwed back on straight, hmmm?"

Cynthia sighed, stuffed a well-used tissue into her pocket and nodded.

"But first hop yourself in the shower and get crackin'. You owe me a brunch."

16

L OOKING OUT THE WINDOW AT THE RUNWAY LINES BLURRING underneath them, Matt exhaled for what seemed like the first time since they'd arrived here two weeks ago, certainly the first time since the Christmas debacle. At the sound, Britney turned to look at him and gave his leg a little squeeze, thinking it was nerves about their impending takeoff.

"It's cool, buddy. We will be up in the air any second, and it'll be smooth sailing 'til we hit Vancouver."

They called each other "buddy." They'd had a very serious discussion early on in their relationship about how they loathed the endearments other people used to refer to their partners: Sweety, Doodle, Cherie ... all awful, and they'd decided the would use "buddy," which they thought unobjectionably cool, oblivious to the disdain of their friends and unaware of the universal fact that any endearment is intolerably lame to anyone on the outside of the union.

"I can't wait," Matt said, smiling. He had been so nervous about bringing Britney, whose parents had decided to spend Christmas at an all-inclusive in Cuba far beyond her price range, home with him for the break. And that was before he had known that his parents had decided to start spending quality time together and he discovered that his mother had lost her mind.

He liked Britney. He truly, completely liked her in that cannot imagine having to spend two weeks away from her kind of way. He maybe loved her. He'd had visions of telling her that while he was home, as they walked amid a flurry of the fat snowflakes and twinkling lights of an Ontario winter, so enchanting in December before the snow turns into clumps of dirty grey ice that render the city a depressing concrete freezer, and its inhabitants become black-wool-clad whiners who make the rest of the country hate them even more than usual.

But in the end he'd said nothing. What could he say? Won't you consider loving me back now that you've seen what a nightmare my family is? He had been mortified about the whole thing, once he'd gotten over being angry. Once he knew that his parents had miraculously managed to avoid messing up the kid, as Abby, for the most part, seemed relieved that the adults' bad behaviour had somehow lessened the impact of her own.

Family relations are just such a danger zone. You never know when someone is going to pull the rug out from under you. You can never just take for granted that it's going to go well. Someone leaves, or they get sick, or they become an idiot when they drink too much, or they just go totally berzerk. The worst scenario he could have imagined before bringing Britney here was nothing compared to what they'd managed to unleash. And she hadn't said a word about it. She must just be counting the seconds until she could get off this plane and the hell away from him.

He looked over at her quietly flipping through a magazine that he knew for a fact she had read at least a dozen times while they sat squirreled away in his dad's basement, in an attempt to prevent any further contact with any member of the family over eighteen.

He knew he had to say something, and if she was gone anyway, he had nothing to lose.

"I'm sorry about the trip," he said as the plane made a shaky ascent.

"You're not the one flying this thing, buddy. It's cool," she said, grabbing his hand, probably thinking he must be a really bad flyer.

"No, I mean the trip here."

"Why? It was nice, I'd never been here before," she said, stroking his hand.

He pulled it away and turned to look at her straight on, a little disappointed that she was putting him through the wringer.

"No, I mean my family. I am so sorry you had to see that. I had no idea they were going to be so awful. I never would have intentionally brought you to something like that, I swear."

"Oh, Christmas? So they had a fight. It happens, no big deal."

"Not a big deal? They had a screaming match in front of all of us at Christmas dinner. I mean, you wouldn't even talk about it after, don't tell me you weren't upset."

"I didn't say anything because I thought it was over. We got back and it all seemed to have settled. I just figured it was a non-issue."

"You don't have to say that, Brit. Please. You don't have to act like it's normal. I want you to know that I know it's not normal." He now took her hand and squeezed it. "I'm not like them."

"Normal? Matt, we haven't had a holiday in years that hasn't ended with my father calling my mother a slut and someone throwing something breakable across the room. I am telling you, that was minor league stuff we saw in there. People fight. At least they tried to fix it. I mean your mom was killing herself trying to be nice to me when we stopped by the house to get the bags, and your dad had his place stocked with everything you like. I mean, look at the stuff they sent us home with?"

"Yeah, but ..." Matt didn't know what to say. "So your family is crazy too?"

"My family is the no-fun dysfunctional kind. I mean, think about it, why did I even come here with you? Because my parents chose to leave town to go to a place I couldn't afford to go to, at Christmas. Your parents flew us both here on your dad's travel points. See the difference?"

"Yeah, but ..."

"Matt. So your family's a bit messed up. They care about you, that much is obvious. And I'm sure it's not all smooth sailing having divorced parents, but trust me it's not great growing up in an emotionally abusive nuclear family either. If you want to get into a saddest childhood competition, I am pretty sure I'd take you."

"You think so?"

"They named me Britney, I win on that alone," she said and leaned over to kiss him. "Trust me, this was the best Christmas I have had maybe ever, and you gave me that, so please don't apologize for it."

"I thought you were going to break up with me," he said, running a hand along her face, still disbelieving that things could possibly work out all right in the end.

Britney laughed, wrinkling her forehead at the sad look on his face, then wrapped his arm around her shoulder, dropping her head on his. "No chance. Wait until you have the pleasure of meeting my family. Then I'll be the one begging you not to run for the hills."

"I think we should just tell them all to shag off and become our own family," Matt said, trying to tell her how he felt about her and unaware that what he'd offered was tantamount to asking her to marry him.

She looked at him oddly for a moment then relaxed back into position. "I love you, too."

17

S TREET PARKING WAS THE WORST, TOM THOUGHT FOR AT least the millionth time as he stood ankle-deep in the dirty snow left behind by the plough's morning run, scraping angrily at the ice on the windshield. How was it that he was currently living in an almost million-dollar home, and he still had to park his damn cars on the street?

"Let's go, Dad. Seriously, if I'm late onto the ice, I'm going to have to skate extra laps.... AGAIN," Ben pleaded from the warmth of the car.

"Well, you won't have to if we end up in an accident because my vision is impaired," Tom hollered back over the music blasting on the stereo, knowing he sounded just like his father, like a crusty old man.

He always felt like an old man when he was out with his younger children. Back when Matt had played city league hockey, Tom had been the coach. He'd be out on the ice reliving his glory days. Now he sat in the stands, often finding himself complaining with the hockey moms about how drafty the older arenas were, how bitter the coffee.

But he did still enjoy it, even watching from the sidelines. The thrill of a last-minute drop in the corner, the cool, cutting sound of blades on the ice, the slap of wood on rubber echoing through the arena. Plus, this was the only time he really had to spend alone with Ben.

Ben had only been a toddler when Tom left, and while he had always had access to the kids, much more than most divorced dads had or wanted, he had never really lived with this son. He had always been the good-time parent but had never helped him with his homework or taken care of him when he was sick. He wondered if his son thought of him as a real father.

Tom worried about this a lot, what effect his absence had on his youngest son, but it was hard to think that anything was wrong with Ben. He was one of those humans, a very rare breed, who seemed to exude contentment. Tom believed the kid was happy, having always at the ready a joke or a sunny smile. And he had the uncanny ability to really listen to you, something that was in terribly short order amongst the rest of them, though Tom saw in him echoes of Cynthia as a little girl.

Ben said little and noticed everything. The kid kept his own counsel, did just well enough in school to avoid real disapproval, threw himself into the physical activities so despised by the others, even Matt, who'd played more to avoid being teased than for a love of competition, and generally kept under the radar. When Tom had the time to think about it, and to be honest it wasn't often, he did worry a little bit about Ben, a kid who, because of his low-key, jokey demeanour, was often left to manage on his own, unheard among the howling demands of his siblings.

After the embarrassing Christmas blow-up, he had heard enough, loud and clear from Matt's psychology 101 criticisms about all of them as humans and Julia's theatrical angry silence and door slamming, to get a sense of what they thought about the family's failed experiment in the art of peacemaking. The fact that they had both decided to spend the remainder of the holidays with Tom was an indication that Cynthia was taking the harshest of their judgment, though they may just have wanted to stay close to Abby. It was nice to see the care they had taken with her during that time; even Matt's girlfriend had shown interest.

Though as for Abby, bless her heart, underneath the new jeans and petty larcenies and oversized vocabulary, she was still just a ten-year-old so terrified at being caught out for what she'd done with the story that all of the accusatory and hateful undertones from the whole debacle seemed to have had no effect on her at all. After spending a few days at her aunt's with her grandmother, who assured her that her life was not over and nothing she'd done could not be undone, Abby had taken the very light scolding she received a few days later from two very guilty parents as some sort of miracle, a get-out-of-jail-free card, and a sign that her dabbling in "normal" childhood culture would lead to nothing but trouble.

She had promptly and unceremoniously dumped the pack of snotty little princesses with whom she'd been such an ill fit and returned to her own eccentric endeavours, now knowing that when she spent her time alone, she really was not missing much.

But Ben, well, nobody knew what he thought of the whole thing. Upon his return from Jayne's, he'd just smiled and made a joke about the current temperature of Toronto's nuclear winter, then kept himself occupied with video games expertly adjusting the sound coming out of his headphones to drown out any fighting or inquiries into his state of well-being until heading off with a friend's parents to a tournament out of town, and he'd only arrived back last night.

Tom was startled out of his reverie by the sound of the horn.

"Seriously, Dad ... I'm going to have to do a million laps now," Ben said, punctuating each word with another blast of the horn.

"Better you than me, kiddo," Tom said, jumping the car. "So how was the tournament?" he asked, trying to pass the time as they snaked their way slowly through the maze of one-way streets up to the arena. Even after all of these years, Tom's small-town brain could simply not grasp that it would always take a half hour to drive a distance of ten minutes in the city, so he never allocated the appropriate amount of time to get anywhere. He just couldn't admit to the frustrating reality that a man with a working (and in his case expensive) vehicle would always feel so trapped.

"Okay. We only made it to the semis, but that's because the goalie's an idiot."

"They say a goalie's only as good as his defencemen, kid," Tom teased.

"I swear, if his wingers were Iron Man and Captain America, that guy couldn't stop a shot. I bet he's why we are being punished with the early morning practice." Ben groaned, trying to stretch his arms out with little success, since his frame took up almost all the space on the passenger side.

"Still," Tom said. "It must have been nice to get out of town."

Ben glanced sideways as if he knew where this was heading.

"I guess, but Ryan snores ... and his farts are the rankest." Ben wrinkled his nose. "Like they could kill a small pet."

An easy out, and Tom was tempted to take it, but having tried out the role of responsible parent over the past few months, he found it now harder than before to abdicate his duties, so he persevered.

"Still, I am guessing you weren't too thrilled with how Christmas turned out this year?"

"Oh, that."

"Yes, that. I'm really sorry that happened, Ben."

"Okay."

"It won't happen again."

"Cool."

They drove in silence for a while, Tom sneaking furtive glances at his son, who was studiously examining his face in the visor mirror.

"That zit is gonna pop hard," Ben murmured to himself just as Tom was gearing up to try and pull him a bit more out of his shell.

Disgusting, Tom thought as he slid his leather glove off with his teeth and bit into the soft skin around his thumbnail. He chewed for a while, waiting for the latest in the world's longest series of red lights to turn before speaking again.

"I guess we just wanted you kids to have a traditional Christmas for once, everybody all together, you know? So you didn't feel torn, I guess."

"Hmmm?" Ben said absently, looking down at his shoes. "Okay. Well, it's over, it's fine," he replied, bringing his own thumb to his mouth, mimicking his father without knowing it. Tom noticed. It was one of the few common traits that indicated they were father and son, Tom a slight but strong dark-haired Irishman, Ben a lanky, sandy blond and dead ringer for his maternal grandfather.

Tom sighed, thinking the conversation had run its course, and was surprised that after a minute, Ben's hand fell to his lap and he said, matter-of-factly, "Us being together isn't a traditional Christmas for me."

Tom felt the weight of parental failure settling upon his shoulders and wondered if maybe it was better when Ben didn't talk. Not better maybe, but easier.

"I know Ben, and we are all so sorry for that." He hit the turn signal as they approached the arena parking lot, sorry that he had finally gotten the boy talking just when they would have to break it up and considering that Ben himself might have planned it that way. Still, it was a real nice way to send the kid out to a practice — he should lend out his services as a depression coach.

"I'm not," Ben said, flashing a smile. "I like having double holidays. That's my tradition…. Ow!" he said, opening up the door and hauling himself out rather ungraciously, cracking his head on the door frame as he did it. To see him on the ice, you'd never guess what a true klutz he could be on solid ground.

It might have been genuine. Ben wasn't known for telling lies or even half-truths successfully, which would do him no favours when he started dating, Tom thought. He inspected his son for tell-tale signs of lying, to see if he was just placating him, since the kid did have charm by the boatload and the ability to say the right thing when someone was feeling down. A quality Tom admired in him. Still, he didn't want Ben to whitewash his feelings about something like this just to make Dad feel better.

"Really?"

"Yeah … can we stop sharing now? I am super duper late," Ben called, making his way around to the trunk of the car.

Tom rolled down his window. "Almost. I just want to know that you're doing okay … I wonder sometimes if you wish ..." Tom knew his time was limited now, but he wasn't sure what he wanted to say. Wish we'd stayed a family? Wish you'd had a full-time dad? Wish it had all been different? "... wish you were like more of your friends?" he finished lamely.

"Dad, all my friends' parents are divorced, this isn't the Middle Ages, or ... you know, the fifties," Ben said from somewhere behind the shiny black steel of the trunk lid.

Tom stepped out of the car, watching his son hoist his enormous hockey bag onto his shoulder. "I just want to make sure that you're happy, I guess.... Don't slam the ... lid," he said too late.

"Sorry," Ben said, and without missing a beat, added, "And that was not acting out, Dr. Phil. I just don't know my own strength." He grinned as he turned towards the arena. "I'm happy, Dad. I'm happy and I'm now really late."

"And I want to say I'm sorry if I wasn't around enough," Tom called to the back of his son's head. "We love you, Jen and I, very much. You know that, right?" He'd said it a little louder than he meant to, noticing one of Ben's tardy teammates casting a glance their way. He also noticed Ben's ears were now an unnatural shade of red.

"Wow ... Dad, what are you doing to me here?" Ben was walking back towards his father in long strides and speaking sharply through his teeth. Tom looked up at his son, nearly as tall as him now, and thought that he might have now lived long enough to see the day that all fathers of sons fear. The day that son kicks their ass. He even closed his eyes, thinking that he was really in no position to fight back.

"Dad, you drive me to practice at seven a.m. every Saturday morning ... well, somewhere around seven, and Jennifer? She washes my hockey gear. *Of course* I know you love me. There is no need to scream about it to me in public places, okay?"

Tom didn't speak, simply bowed his head in apology and left Ben to run ahead into the arena. He silently thanked any and all of the deities that had played a part in sending him such a great kid. When he finally made it into the stands to where a few of the hockey moms were hanging out, they remarked at how chipper he was so early in the morning.

Tom sat on the cold wooden bench through the whole practice, amazed at the skill Ben displayed on the ice. He really was graceful, but never afraid to take or give a good hit, but he was also always the first one to offer a hand up or a pat on the back. The kid really was a gentleman. Tom was so focused on his son's ownership of the ice that he didn't notice Cynthia's arrival until he heard one of the women he was sitting with say: "That's Ben's mother ... I know, that's because she *never* comes."

These women, who had dedicated so many cold, uncomfortable hours to their son's hypothetical future careers, had very little time for "playoff parents," the ones who only showed up twice a year bundled like they were on an Arctic voyage and bringing in lattes from the fancy coffee shop around the corner. Cynthia was the consummate playoff parent.

Tom watched her slowly make her way around the arena, stopping to wave vigorously at Ben, who would surely be mortified, her eyes then scanning the stands, presumably looking for Tom. She never showed up at the arena, and he was both nervous and curious.

She spied him and started up the steps.

"Oh, hi again," said one of the mothers far too sweetly.

"Oh, yes, hi," Cynthia replied distractedly.

"I'm Patty, Justin's mom?"

"Yes, of course, hi."

"And you're Ben's mom ... Cyndi, is it?"

"Close, Cynthia."

"Oh, so sorry, it's just that we never see you here, just Tom and his wife, so I forgot, you see."

"Right, no problem," Cynthia said, shifting her gaze up to Tom, an eyebrow raised in a plea for some assistance.

"I should have remembered, since you have that show, but I just can't stand that station. No offence, it's just too politic-y, no fun."

"Well, I guess news isn't for everyone," Cynthia said, an edge creeping into her voice.

Tom was enjoying this immensely, and it was doing a great job of cutting the mounting tension he'd been feeling as she approached. He hadn't seen her since she'd left his house on Christmas, and he had assumed that they were choosing to deal with the situation in their usual manner of not dealing with it.

"And you'll remember Ryan's mom, of course. She's the one that took your Ben to the tournament over the holidays? I believe you were too busy now that you've all decided to go back to work?"

Ryan's mother smiled coldly. "It has been a while," she said, not extending her hand.

"Mmmhmmm. Very busy." Cynthia's expression had morphed from one of embarrassment to one of severe irritation, and Tom decided that she had probably suffered enough at the hands of this fleece-wearing pack of wolves.

"Is one of those for me?" he said, pointing at the elegant paper cups in her hands.

Cynthia hopped up the final stair, her arm extended. "Oh, yes. I thought you might like this instead of the crap that passes for coffee in these places." She looked innocently at the women below her, all holding Styrofoam cups. "Oh. No offence."

Tom coughed to cover a laugh and pulled her up a few more rows, giving them a bit of privacy. "Let's avoid another brawl, shall we?" he said as they sat down.

"What a bunch of bitches," Cynthia said as she arranged her coat and keys. She looked up at the clock. "I guess that's what you get at such an ungodly hour."

"I was going to drop him off, Cyn. I always do."

"I know. I just thought that maybe we should talk a little. Perhaps clear the air a bit? And figured that was probably best done in a public place. And I figured this would be the best place to find you on your own. I tried calling your wife to apologize for my, ahem, outburst, and realize that we will probably not be having tea again any time soon."

"Yes, well. She was a little upset."

"Yeah, well, in my defence, I was too. But I'm not actually here to talk about that. I mean, let's face it, she and I were never going to be best of friends anyway, right?"

They were talking to each other, staring straight at the ice and watching as the other kids headed for the changerooms, leaving only Ben to skate lonely circles around the perimeter, glancing up occasionally at the two of them, a perturbed look on his face.

"No. I can't say I envision that," he said dryly.

"But, you know I do hope that didn't cause you guys any real problems."

"No. Cooler heads prevailed in the morning. You did get me signed up for another round of couples therapy though. So thanks for that," Tom smiled. "Not that we couldn't use it, I guess."

"Well, good. I'm glad to hear it." And it sounded to Tom like she really was.

"So what is it you wanted to ..."

"I am not in love with you," Cynthia jumped in.

"Oh. Well. Good for you." Tom hadn't really thought that she was, and didn't really want her to be, but still, hearing her say it, he was strangely affronted.

"I mean, that story. That wasn't 'I love you now,' It was 'I loved you then' … Honestly it was more that I loved at all. You see?" Cynthia said, tapping her fingers on the cup in her hand.

"Not really."

"I just need to know that you know that I am not on some insidious hunt to win you back, okay?"

"Okay."

"We were not meant to be together. Not forever. And it's taken me a really long time to admit it, because to admit it means that I'd have to admit that us breaking up was probably something that would have happened anyway, and I've been afraid to even think it, because it somehow endorses what you did to me, Tom. And it was shitty, it was a shitty, horrible, heartbreaking thing that you did."

"I know that, Cynthia. And I am sorry."

"I hated you for a long time for moving on and getting to start a new life like you did. I couldn't say it, wouldn't ever say it, because of the kids and also because of my pride. But I've been thinking about this a lot the past few weeks. I suppose in the aftermath of total humiliation one gets somewhat reflective, but I need to stop blaming you for moving on with your life, and I really need to stop blaming you for why I didn't move on with mine."

She said it so quietly, he could barely hear her over the noises in the creaky old barn, and she never looked at him once. He wanted desperately to take hold of her hand, to help her through this somehow, but he knew that wasn't what she'd want. It was the perfect example of why they would have fallen apart anyway. He could see it now too.

"I got so wrapped up in the kids, they seemed the safest bet to make sure I didn't ever go through something like that again. But they are growing up so fast, so unbelievably fast, and all of a sudden I have come out of this life of parenting and realized I have nothing but a job that I sadly fell out of love with too, somewhere along the way, probably when I stopped having stories of my own to tell, and I started mining theirs to fill the air. I am glad to have the job, don't get me wrong, I'm not going anywhere. I appreciate what it has given me, but it's not enough. Not the way I've been doing it, anyway.

"And then Abby shows up, so sweet, so full of enthusiasm and life, looking to me for help, and I get this wonderful opportunity to dive headlong back into my old comfortable patterns. But I'm drowning in the nostalgia here, I know it. I never should have written that piece, and I'm sorry."

"Please don't be sorry," Tom said after taking a long drink to loosen the tightness in his throat. "It's beautiful, Cyn, and it's honest." He turned towards her eyes, cast down at her cup. "And please don't sit here and tell me you've wasted your life. First of all you have raised three great kids. I mean, I love them with all of my heart, no one can say you loved them more than me, but I know that I wasn't there for them the way that you were, the way I should have been. And I know the reason why they are the kind of people I am proud to say I know is you. So don't question the value of that. Second, you are forty-five, not eighty. Life is not over yet and there are still plenty of stories for you to write. You've got the talent, you just need the material."

She shot a look up at him with a small smile. "Easier said than done."

"I don't know about that. You've caused quite a splash amongst the family, and managed to alienate a few more people here today, maybe you can create a new genre, 'aggressive memoir.'"

"It's a thought, but I think I'll pass so as to ensure that there is at least some hope that those children that you think I raised so well will continue to speak to me."

"You aren't willing to suffer for your art? You're no Dorothy Parker," Tom said with a grin.

"Ha. How is Abby? It was sweet of her to write me that apology letter. I hope she got mine in return."

"Yes. She's fine. She's no longer dressing like a hooker, which I for one find quite refreshing."

"Has she given up on writing?"

"No chance, if it's not in the genes, maybe she's getting it osmosis-style from Matt's leftover clothing."

"Well, I know lessons are off the table, rightly so. But if she ever wants a little advice, I'm willing to share, while supervised by a responsible sibling or adult."

"I'll let her know."

"Thanks."

Tom looked up to see Ben climbing the stairs, still in his skates, and Tom felt the moment was about to pass and never present itself again, so he stood quickly, taking Cynthia's elbow to help her up.

"For the record, I will always love you, Cyn. You were the best friend I ever had. You were just too good for me."

"You got that right," she said, blushing as she stepped away from him slightly.

The clatter of metal on concrete filled the silence until Ben reached the top of the stairs. "Please tell me we are not all going out for breakfast."

"I promise. I just thought I would come pick you up so you can get a nice early start on the project you're supposed to have finished for science class on Friday," Cynthia said, turning him around back towards the dressing room. "And I am no expert, but I am pretty sure you are ruining those blades. Let's go."

Ben started down the stairs, turning back to give his dad a quick wave. "I never thought I'd say it, but science is better than brunch."

18

JULIA SHIFTED UNCOMFORTABLY IN THE BACK SEAT OF THE car, desperately in need of a trip to the washroom but unwilling to go until Cynthia had finished. The battle royal between them still raged on, and the only reason Julia found herself tolerating prolonged time in the presence of her mother, essentially ruining her March Break, was the necessity of a ride to go and visit her future home. As she watched Cynthia growing smaller through the windshield, she realized she'd been holding her breath and let it out in a huge whoosh, wriggling again to find some comfort and secretly urging her mother to hurry up.

"I don't care how angry you are at present, honey, let me be clear here, these are leather seats, and I'm not going to have you pissing all over them, so get on out and go to the can, will you?" Ellen said, staring into the rearview mirror, the effort of turning around seemingly beyond her.

The women were day two into this road trip, and Ellen had already inferred her breaking point had been reached with the shenanigans of the dueling Wilkes. She had been comforted to some extent by assurances from both the other two, offered whenever a private minute allowed, that without her presence they would have probably killed each other by now, but it was becoming clear that she wondered if it was worth sacrificing her sanity to keep them alive.

———⟫•◦•⟪———

"It'll be fun," Cynthia had promised weeks earlier when she first mentioned the trip. A girls' adventure. "We'll be like Thelma and Louise."

"Why do people always say that like it's a good thing? Has no one ever watched the whole movie?" Ellen inquired. "Though you've got your roles down, I'd guess. I'd just get billing as 'terrified innocent bystander.'"

"Please, El, this is the only leverage I have to make her spend any time at all with me, and if you don't come, I'm honestly afraid it will be just another utter disaster," Cynthia said in that pleading way that so impacted and annoyed Ellen. "It may be the last chance I have to reach out to her before she goes. You know she got hired back at that camp this summer, and she's got half her damn bags already packed."

———⟫•◦•⟪———

So there Ellen sat, stuck in the car after another annoying whinge-fest between the two of them, this time over the music selection, which was utterly ridiculous, since everybody in the world knows that the driver DJs, and no

one was getting behind the wheel of Ellen's Mercedes —
a fortieth birthday present from herself and her mother's
estate — but Ellen.

"Fine ... but gawd, Ellen she's just so ..."

"Just so the woman who gave birth to you and raised
you and is taking a week's vacation to drive halfway across
the country to give you a sneak peek at the college she is
going to drop an insane amount of money to send you to for
the next four years, just to make you happy?"

"I was going to say difficult," muttered Julia, but she
smiled. Julia would, it had been argued, lip off to anyone
including the Lord Almighty himself, but she never tried
it with Ellen. While her feelings towards her mother were
tumultuous at times and complicated always, how she felt
about Ellen was black and white. She loved her undyingly.
Ellen was the best.

"You're the mother I should have had," Julia said leaning
forward, a compliment, but also a nod to the fact that she
was not yet ready to completely let go of the mom-bashing.

"One, you have the mother you should have had, and
two you did also have me, and so you are one lucky so and
so, and don't you forget it. Now seriously, get out of the car,
Jules, you are grabbing at your crotch like a five-year-old, or
a pop star. Either way it's not very attractive."

Julia was about to protest when her phone indicated
another text message, one of the hundreds that had been
punctuating their conversations and silences with notification
chimes at the rate of one a minute. She looked at the screen,
swore under her breath, and popped out of the door, thumbs
moving frantically as she walked, narrowly missing the car
pulling into the gas pump beside them.

what do u want?

anthr chnce.

To be a dillweed?

Lol. cum on I said sorry.

And I said no way. Give it up.

She was about to hit the send button when a last minute change of heart caused her to delete the last half and fire it off.

Jesse had been back on the periphery for weeks now and all of a sudden had begun making a play to take her to prom. He desperately wanted to go with her, it seemed. He'd approached her at parties, left notes at her locker, burned her a number of CDs filled with apologetic arena rock anthems. The other day she'd found a rather cheezy velveteen beanbag mouse on her desk, which, though in honour of a nickname she actually despised, she'd been touched to see he remembered.

Now the texting campaign was in full force. Would she please consider accompanying him? As a couple, as friends, as angry acquaintances, however Julia wanted to play it. The way he told it, he'd been missing her a lot since she'd broken up with him in the fall. He realized he should have been more mature about everything, and now that they were looking at the last few weeks of school together, he had decided it was time to make amends.

She had been genuinely surprised to find his words and gestures were sincere, more surprised to find out that they might be working on her. But he'd been a total jerk, betrayed her publicly, and she had already determined that there was no way she was going to be interested in somebody like that. Not when she was weeks away from the freedom of a whole new life. Still, the idea that the texts would stop made her antsy. Plus, due to the rather convincing ice queen persona she'd taken on over the last semester, she had become an even more powerful and terrifying adolescent idol, but because of it no one else had had the balls to ask her to the damn dance. She was currently dateless, and all the good options were quickly being snapped up by her friends. It could be very lonely at the top.

She felt the vibration of the phone throughout her body when she saw the response: *Fine have it ur way. I'm dun.*

But it might just have been her stomach dropping out.

With her eyes glued to the screen, staring unhappily at his response, Julia didn't see her mother, who was walking towards her, nose buried in her own electronic device as she checked in on things at home.

From the car, Ellen watched the impending collision with resigned good humour. "Unbelievable."

"Ow!"

"Dammit, Julia," Cynthia said, rubbing her shin then laughing at the consequences of their shared bad habits. Julia burst into tears.

It was a shock to them both. Julia didn't cry, ever. When angry, she raged, when elated, she shouted, and she preferred to deal with all the tricky emotions somewhere far away from the prying eyes and concerns of those around her. But there, in the parking lot of a dirty gas station in eastern Quebec, there were simply too many stuffed in her hidey hole, and she could no longer tell where one ended and another began, much less sort them out. A general anger towards her mother; excitement masking terror about what her future may hold in the coming months; and of course her attraction that equalled the distrust she felt for the boy, who despite all of her protests and protective armour, she had let get close enough to bruise her heart again. So she gave up trying and just let them run out, tears streaming down her face.

"Oh, honey, I'm sorry. Are you hurt?" Cynthia said, instinctively reaching out for her daughter, who instinctively let her.

"He asked me to prom, and I said no, and I don't even want to go, and now I can't and I hate him!" Julia wailed into her mother's shoulder.

Cynthia cast a bewildered look in the direction of the car, shrugging. Through the glass she watched Ellen shake her head slowly before throwing open the door and stepping out.

"What's up?"

"A boy. I think," Cynthia said between soothing shushes and there, theres.

"Of course it is. What's the story, kiddo?" Ellen asked, raising a hand to stroke Julia's hair.

Overtired, overstressed, and centred between her moms, Julia let it all out. She told them about Jesse, and the note, and the break-up and the months of frosty silence and the impossibility of finding someone you could really count on and how angry she was that she couldn't stop caring about this stupid idiot of a boy.

"Well, it sounds to me like you really like this Jesse kid," said Ellen rather matter-of-factly. "You might as well tell him he can take you and see how it goes."

Julia looked up at Ellen, red-eyed. "But he was a total selfish jerk," she said, turning towards her mother for support. Cynthia, who would gladly mow down Jesse in the street for the upset he had caused her baby, hesitated before responding.

It was her right to pray that her daughter would never, ever be hurt, her desire to do everything in her power to keep her safe. But it was her job to make sure that she did feel things, to make sure that Julia was an active participant in her own life, something she knew that she had not shown her by example.

Because it was her job to make sure that her kids had the tools they needed to be happy. And the sad and true fact was that in this life, you don't get the sweet without the sour. She didn't want Julia to ever be afraid that she couldn't get hurt and still go on. She didn't want her to get stuck like she had.

"Honey, he's eighteen years old," Ellen continued, seemingly less conflicted, but then Ellen had always thrown her chips in and left life up to fate. "At eighteen, they're all selfish jerks. At least this one said sorry."

"Mom?" Julia asked, wanting to hear from her, needing her. Cynthia wondered briefly how sick it was that she was taking any pleasure in this, but shoved it aside, a guilt to chew on another day, and squeezed her daughter tighter.

"I know it's hard, honey, but you have to trust yourself. If you like him, and you believe he's sorry, and you think you'd have a good time with him, then you should go with that. Look at you, you're about to set off on a whole new chapter of your life. Why not just let go a little and enjoy the friends you have now while you've got the chance? "

Julia had calmed down and was wiping the tears from her face. "Well, it's too late now, anyway. I don't think he's going to ask again, and I'm certainly not going to ask him. That's *never* going to happen."

"That's so retro," Ellen said disgustedly, grabbing the phone out of Julia's hand. "Get the kid up on this gizmo for me."

"No!" Julia shouted, grabbing at the phone. "What would you say?"

"Nothing uncool, don't you worry about that," Ellen said, holding it just out of Julia's reach. "If he's been doing all you say he's been doing, all you need to say is …"

"What time are you picking me up?" Cynthia finished, finding herself swayed by the teen-movie-tone drama of it all.

"No way." Julia grabbed the phone, looking at them both. "Really?"

"It's cool, kid, he'll bite," Ellen said.

Julia stood there thumbs at the ready, waiting.

"Come on, you're miserable already... what have you got to lose?"

She fired out the message and sent it off. "Oh ... if he says no ..."

"He won't," said Ellen.

"I'll die if he says no ..." Julia said, her cheeks flushed and her voice high.

"No one would be foolish enough to let you get away twice," said Cynthia, hugging her daughter again.

"Ahhh, lame, Mom." But she didn't move away.

There was no immediate response. They stood staring at each other for a long minute, then to break the mounting tension, Ellen shouted, "Let's get this show on the road," and herded them back into the car. Just as they were pulling off the exit, they heard the chime. From the rearview mirror they could see the grin.

"What's it say?" Cynthia asked, feeling somehow victorious.

"Nothing," Julia said, and Cynthia sighed slightly as she watched things slowly shift back to normal.

"A good nothing?" asked Ellen.

"Ummm yeah ... thanks." Thumbs flying once again.

"Ah. The healing power of a feminine heart-to-heart," Ellen said, steering the car back onto the highway, and gave a stereo knob a twist. "So we're all friends again and don't we all feel better."

"Oh hell! No!" came the distressed reply from the backseat.

"That little son of a ..." Cynthia was already plotting the pain which she could legally inflict on Jesse his friends and relations, but Julia continued.

"I didn't pee. You have got to pull over."

"Honey, we just got on the highway. You are going to have to hold it," Cynthia said, laughing rather unsympathetically in her relief.

"I don't think I can."

"You two are seriously working my last nerve," Ellen said, slowing down the car and pulling off to the side of the highway. "Out you go."

"You want me to pee on the highway?" asked Julia.

"We're twenty minutes at least from the next stop, so it's either the highway or the seats, and if it's the seats, you're a dead woman. Just head down the gulley. There's some shrubbery down there and the tissue box is behind you ... Unless you can hold it?"

Urgency won out. Julia grabbed the box and stared to scrabble down the incline, scanning furtively for possible voyeurs.

Cynthia watched her drop down behind the shrubs. "Oh god, El. Sometimes it's nice to remember how awful it was to be young, isn't it?"

"You said it. Though let's face it, she's heading off to university, this will not be the last time she pees in the bushes. At least she'll have some practice."

19

"WRITE WHEN YOU ARE FEELING SORRY FOR YOURSELF, by all means," his mother told him once, during a rather intense period of pubescent blues. "But do yourself and the rest of the world a favour and don't try to get it published." Looking at the screen shimmering in its constant state of refreshment, he could grudgingly concede her point.

> *Who can be optimistic of the fate that lies ahead*
> *Half strangled in the workman's noose, sick*
> *stomach, throbbing head*
> *Whatever noble dreams I had so hopefully set*
> *out for me*
> *I'll numb from causing any pain with pills*
> *and lukewarm whiskey*
> *I know within the soulless box in which I waste*
> *my sands of time*
> *I'm farther from the life I want than when I*

opened up my eyes
I push farther into weeks and month and years
of average pay
Passed from boss to bank to barman as I drink
my cares away
Endless compromises lead to comfort sought
through vice
As I smoke and screw and ask anew
"What happened to the artist's life?"

It was embarrassing. He could see that, plainly reassessing what he'd so bitterly typed up only a few hours before, though at the time he'd felt it to be so therapeutically and painfully honest, so acutely real. It was poetry first of all, never his strong suit. On top of that it was whiney and melodramatic, without any sense of grandeur. It was boring. Reading it again, he could almost see himself on a wooden stool at some crap-hole coffee shop that fancied itself "gritty" but was merely unclean, proselytizing in a drawn-out monotone to a group of other emotional sadists waiting for their turn as he gazed out a grimy window, hoping for greater impact.

"Ugh," he said, hitting the delete key on the already highlighted text and shoving himself away from the memory of the offending words with enough force that his chair rolled out into the hallway, a wheel catching the corner of one of the many cardboard boxes lining the wall and almost tipping him over.

"Dude," Kevin admonished, "watch my stuff, will you? I'll be gone soon enough."

Impending graduation, along with Britney's near-constant presence at the apartment and a long-suffered though unmentioned resentment at what Kevin saw as Matt's "obsessive" need to clean the apartment every week, had led Kevin to decide the time was right to strike out on his own.

This coincided nicely with Matt accepting a position working for a local weekly news magazine, which made up for its rather paltry starting salaries with the promise of getting to write for a living, creating the perfect opportunity for Britney, who still had two years of school left, to take over Kevin's room and for them to try out full-time coupledom. A roommate upgrade, freedom from academic commitments, and gainful employment. The happiness trifecta for most new graduates … yet Matt was feeling morose. So down, in fact, that in the vein of many angry young men before him, he'd taken to writing terrible poetry.

What really bothered him was that he hadn't even wanted the damn nomination. He had been very much swayed by Britney's view of the elite elements that clung like burrs to academic life. Plus, he knew he'd been a total long shot from the beginning. Still painfully shy, he'd hardly ever engaged with any of his department cohorts outside of required group projects and the occasional opportunity to take advantage of a faculty-funded free bar, and yet still he found the news that he had not been chosen as a recipient of the Dean's Achievement Award had found a chink in the armour he had so painstakingly built around his professional pride. It had instantly erased all of the delight he'd experienced upon learning that one of his professors had taken enough notice of him, of his work, to put his name forward in the first place.

He could not believe that he'd let his hopes get so high over the possibility of winning that he'd made the uncharacteristic and foolish mistake of counting pre-hatched eggs. He'd even begun drafting his acceptance speech, something he'd intended to be inspiring and witty, a humble (but not too humble) story of his journey from a young, unsure kid to a passionate self-made artist who had shed his past to build his future. Something that would show his parents, his mother particularly, how far he had come and what he could accomplish.

Except he hadn't been chosen, so he'd deleted that particular piece of fiction, replacing it with expressions of despondency ever since. He had also opted out of the graduation ceremony due to his growing shame at having cared about any of this at all. The news had not been taken well by either of his parents, particularly since he hadn't told them about the nomination, envisioning instead their fierce and teary pride when he nonchalantly presented them with the convocation program, his name displayed in a prominent font among the other winners. However, since they were both still trying to mend fences with their oldest child before they lost him to the man he was so rapidly becoming, they hadn't pushed it.

"Sorry, Kev. Wouldn't want to risk cracking the spines on any of those textbooks you never touched in four years." Matt had intended it as a joke, but even to him it sounded like cheap shot. "Sorry. I think I need to get out of here for a bit."

Heading for the door, he saw that Britney had brought up the mail. He knew it was her, since neither he or Kevin ever remembered to check the slot, the reason why they had found their land line service had been cut off due to lack of payment on more than one occasion. It was amazing to him the things that girls just seemed to know innately to do. Remembering to check the mail, buying new dish soap when the old bottle was running low, closing the windows before it rained or putting things back in the place they belonged every time. He was both excited and terrified about the organizational transformation that would take place once Kevin was gone and Britney had free rein over the place.

He saw the bright purple envelope on the tray, covered in Abby's signature glitter horse stickers. It is a rare occurrence, sadly getting rarer, to receive fun mail via the post, and no matter how low you are laid, it can't help but cheer you up. The first genuine smile Matt had mustered in weeks crossed his face as he picked up the vibrant rectangle stuffed too thick for its small size, and shoved it in his back pocket.

He walked past the convenience store below his place, feeling sorry, not for the first time, that he'd never cottoned on to smoking. He couldn't stand the smell of it, and did truly believe it could kill you, but he couldn't deny that there was something so coolly and beautifully evocative of a person's sadness and isolation expressed in the way some people held a cigarette, the wisps of smoke escaping from their nostrils. Today would be a good day to have a cigarette in the park. Instead he bought a pack of black licorice, feeling even more of an artistic failure, and headed to the parkette up the street, a place he often went to read and think or to people watch for inspiration.

He opened the envelope and pulled out a photocopied four-sheet newsletter along with a handwritten note.

> Dear Matt,
> CONGRATULATIONS!!! I am so proud of you and hope you are having fun writing at your new job. I am glad you are coming home soon. I have been writing too like you said I should. My teacher put one story I wrote in our school newspaper!! Your mom helped me write this one and I think it's

pretty good. She said it's like the mystery stories you used to write as a kid. (But I made this one up all by myself I PROMISE!!!!) I hope you think it's good too. I can't wait to see you and Britney and to show you some of my other stories.

Love you and miss you!!

Abby

P.S. Dad and Mom and Ben say "hi." Julia says "whatever."

XXOO

A

He picked up the school paper, impressed by the drawing on the front page, which seemed too good to have been drawn by some eighth grader, and skimmed the pages looking for Abby's story. He was proud to see it ran the full back page. He actually felt a tear in the corner of his eye when he saw that she'd dedicated it to him.

The Three Oakes Mystery

By Abigail Wilkes

For Matthew Wilkes

Tim and Jenna Watson loved their new mansion with its lush green lawns, tropical pools and three large oak trees; sure to be a hit with their kids Matt (12) and Ben (11). The minute they saw them it was:

"Can I climb them, Mom? Plee-eeaasee."

"Me too Mom me too!"

"Oh alright," said Jenna. "But don't be late for dinner." She went inside and so did Tim.

A half hour later the boys ran in breathless and said they found a wooden box and inside was a map. What they didn't know yet was that it was a map that Robert Crossen had been looking for.

The map had belonged to Crossen's family for generations until they went bankrupt and were forced to sell the mansion. Crossen had sworn that one day he would find the map that led to a treasure that his first ancestor, Ichabod Crossen, was rumored to have hid in an African village.

When the Watsons discovered that what the boys had found in the Oak tree was a treasure map, they read it and began to make plans, eager to go after the treasure and swearing each other to secrecy. They did not know they were being watched and that Robert Crossen had found out their plan and was making some of his own.

As the Watsons boarded the plane to Africa, Robert slid slyly on board as well keeping a close eye on the family for the whole trip.

The plane touched down hours later and Crossen covertly slipped off the plane, waited for the Watsons, and followed them to their hotel where they freshened up and started on the trail.

As they neared what he believed was the final destination he realized the ravine would be a perfect place to get rid of them but it was too soon. He needed them to

take him all the way. He followed closely
and was not seen until they entered a big
cave. He was watching so closely that he
did not see the big rock in front of him.
He stumbled over it and fell to the ground
yelling before passing out. The Watsons
turned quickly and saw that he was injured.
Unaware of his dastardly intentions they
took care of him until he came to. When he
awoke and saw how kind they had been, he
told them what he was doing and said they
shouldn't have wasted their time on him.
But the Watsons forgave him and said there
would be enough treasure for everyone
and if he helped them find it and behaved
himself from then on they could split it.
He thanked them asking only to keep his
family jewels.

Together they went over the hills,
through tunnels and around rivers until
they came to a pit where the treasure was
hidden. As they dug out the treasure they
didn't see the snakes that were encircling
them. Suddenly Ben looked up he screamed.
Everybody froze in their tracks. The only
reason they survived was that Robert had a
flute. (He had thought of this beforehand
having been to Africa as a child.) He played
for half an hour — the most terrifying half
hour of their lives — until finally the snakes
went to sleep. Silently they grabbed the
massive treasure and when they were out
of the pit they ran all the way to the rental

car, back to the airport and on a plane back home. They gave Robert back his family jewels and parted as friends.

About a week later Jenna went into the backyard and looked at the Oak trees wondering what other adventures would come their way.

... That has yet to be seen.

Matt was sitting on the bench, the paper folded in his lap, when Britney found him. She dropped down beside him, grabbing a string of licorice.

"Kevin said, and I quote, 'Matt is being a little bitch,'" she said, patting his arm.

"Yeah, I was. But I think I'm over that now."

"Really?"

"Really," he said, passing her the paper and directing her to Abby's story. "Abby wrote this, for real this time."

She took a few minutes reading it over. "It's pretty good."

"Yeah, I know."

"I mean, even with the phallus jokes aside, it's still pretty good stuff."

"She loves doing it," Matt said. "I mean, she just really loves it. You know."

"Well, buddy, I think that you do too, when you're not always trying to do it for somebody else."

"Yeah. But in the end you're always doing it for someone else, aren't you? I mean, if you didn't want other people to see it, you wouldn't be writing it down. I wish that wasn't the case."

Britney sat, back chewing thoughtfully on her licorice, oblivious to the fact that it was staining her mouth black, which Matt found oddly attractive.

"Well, maybe you are just picking the wrong audience, you know? Stop trying to write for your professors, or your boss … especially your mom, all the people who you think you have to prove something to." She passed the newspaper back to him, pointing to his name at the top. "She wrote this for you. Why don't you try writing one for her and see if that doesn't get a little of the joy flowing?"

20

CYNTHIA WAS EXHAUSTED. SHE HAD BEEN UP SINCE THE crack of dawn cleaning the house and picking up all of Matt's favourite foods for the dinner she was hosting tonight to honour the return of her firstborn, a university graduate with a job lined up already at a small paper out west. She was thrilled for him, and conscious that she was only going to have him home for a limited time. She had even persuaded him that it was safe to bring Britney back to the province and was looking forward for a chance to make a less terrifying impression.

She had resorted to offering them shared accommodations, to the ire of her own mother, to sway him to stay at the house with her. And this time everything was going to be perfect. With Julia headed away to the east coast in September, this would surely be the last time she'd have all of her children with her under one roof, unless they all fell victim to the quarter-life crises that send so may kids back to the nest, and let's face it, no one wants the kids back then.

Over the winter, in an attempt to find something that might make her more than just a working mother, Cynthia had finally taken the plunge into making some of her dream dinners a reality, signing up for classes first at the local grocery store, then at the college in her neighbourhood. Through the classes, she found that while she was a disastrous baker, she had a real knack for the carefree experimentation needed to turn average meals into something really special, and she couldn't wait to show it off.

She had been cooking for the past two days and was only taking a break now because of the guests who had settled themselves in the kitchen. Tom, who had stopped by to pick up Ben to take along for the ride to the airport, had dropped off Abby, who Jennifer had allowed, after several days of pleading and a number of therapy sessions, to attend the welcome-home dinner, while Jennifer herself declined the invitation, which suited all parties concerned.

Sitting with Cynthia in the kitchen now, nibbling on a few of the multitude of appetizers loaded on the table, was Ellen, who had not as yet met the little girl and who, for all her cautions and condemnations, had been equally interested in the meeting.

Cynthia had dropped into a chair between them and was listening to Ellen's latest rant about the never-ending re-organization that had besieged her department since the fall.

"As if I am going to have to go and work out a whole new schedule because some guy from television got bumped and is sniffing around. And they are trying to use it as some sore of leverage? I am too old for this crap. So I said to him, if I am going to have to do some ass-kissing to save my job, the ass I start with sure as hell won't be yours."

"Ellen." Cynthia nodded towards Abby sitting at the other end of the table, her cheeks puffed to bursting with mini cheddar buns. Abby was fascinated by Ellen's big voice and big gestures and had been following her like a puppy since she walked into the house.

"Honey, do you watch TV?"

Abigail nodded, looking at Ellen as though offended by the implication that she might not. "Of course I do," she said through a wall of soggy dough. "My dad has the premium cable."

"Yeah? Well, he would. Cyn, if the girl is watching cable, I think I'm pretty safe saying 'ass' then, aren't I? Or Abby, perhaps you are a fan of the Eastern Zone channels — would you prefer I say 'arse'?" Ellen growled the last part in her best Newfoundland accent, which was really not very good at all.

Abby giggled anyway, and the initial implied slight was forgiven as she bunched up the sleeves of the too-large sweatshirt. She was wearing another from Matt's collection, this one left behind over the Christmas break.

"Honest to god, you are a menace. I should just pack you up a thermos of wine and send you away. You are a bad influence." Cynthia laughed, though she was fairly certain this little "arse" incident would be repeated at home, leading to a pointed email from Jennifer about Cynthia's role in promoting delinquency. Then again, what was another nail in that coffin?

"Too bad for you, sister, but you can't evict family."

Abigail's head popped up from her inspection of the next object of consumption. Of course she had been listening, drinking in every word like a sponge, and Cynthia regretted the wine joke now too. "You guys are family?" Abby asked.

"Uh-huh." Ellen nodded. "No shaking me. I've been in the fold since 1987."

"Nineteen eighty-seven?" Abby stopped, her eyes screwed up as she did the math. "But you are too old."

"Ain't that the truth." Ellen tipped her glass towards the little girl in amusement. "But what's your point?"

"Well, you can't be cousins or anything if you only met then. Right?" While Cynthia had a sister with kids, Tom and Jennifer were both only children, leaving Abby with no cousins.

"We aren't related by blood, honey, you're right. Ellen and I met at work and became fast friends."

"Then you are not family?"

"We are a different kind of family. A better kind. The kind you pick yourself." Ellen stood and walked over to the counter in search of a top-up for her wine.

"El, dinner's not for at least another hour ... you are going to be asleep by then."

"Just a top-up, Mother, today was a real shit-show. Oh, hell. Okay, Abby, for that one I am sorry. Don't swear, don't do drugs, and stay in school. Oops ... maybe I'll make it a half glass," Ellen said, tipping more wine on the counter than back into the bottle. "I think I'm going to sit in the comfy seats, away from temptation."

When Ellen had passed through the kitchen door, Abigail, in her usual machine-gun approach to conversation, looked at Cynthia and asked: "Are we family?"

"What? Er ... pardon.. What?"

"Are we family. You and me?" The second time the question was louder and the look in her eyes both shy and pleading. Cynthia stood up, trying not to pace.

"God, kid, what a loaded question," Ellen chimed in from the living room.

"Not helpful, Ellen," Cynthia called back, her mind racing with a decade's worth of unanswerable questions and recently excavated emotional wreckage. Who was this little girl to her?

Not getting a reply in due time, Abby asked another. "Do you love me?"

The question took up too large a space in the room, silent but for Ellen's slow-approaching footsteps. "Well, do you like me at least?" Abigail quickly retreated to safer ground, an act of self-defence. This kid. What could Cynthia do with this friggin' kid who just repeatedly ripped her heart out, who wanted so damn much.

"Oh honey, of course she likes you," Ellen said, elbowing Cynthia sharply in the ribs, startling her out of her own head. "Hell, I like you, and I don't even like kids."

"Of course. Of course I do, Abby," Cynthia parroted. Noticing that she was wringing her hands as she said it, she quickly dropped them to her sides. "Yes, I like you. Obviously."

This established, Abby began to present her case. "Well, we even have the same people in our families," she said, shooting an accusatory look at no-relation Ellen.

"Touché, kid." Cynthia heard the sound of ice against glass as Ellen moved on to the harder stuff. "Got a bit of the lawyer in her, that one."

"I'm a writer," Abby said before rhyming off a list of communal kin. "Matt and Ben and Julia."

"Yes."

"My dad."

"Er … well…"

"Isn't he still your family?"

"Jeez, you're right, looks like we have a cub reporter on our hands here. Too bad there'll be no media left worth a damn to work for by the time she's ready."

"Seriously, Ellen, not the time … your dad … honey … that's hard to say."

"Well, you still have Gramma over for visits. Even for her birthday. I've heard her say so."

"You're right, I do."

"So that makes Gramma your family, right?"

"I suppose."

"And you aren't even related to her either." Abigail dropped the trump card.

"True."

"Yeah. Well, I just thought maybe I could be that kind of family too."

"Oh." Cynthia tried to put a choke-hold on her emotions, acutely aware now that she had the power rip out Abby's heart too, but over the past few months, Cynthia had blown that dam, and she found herself very near tears.

"It's okay," Abby said, trying to sound indifferent and shifting her gaze back to the food on the table, though she didn't reach for anything. "You probably already have too much … I just … I don't. And so I … just …"

"Oh, please don't cry, kiddo." Ellen turned to Cynthia with the eyes of a stern mother. "Fix this," she hissed through her teeth. "You are totally killing my buzz. Abby, don't cry. Of course you can be that kind of family. No doubt about it."

"Yes, of course, honey, we are family." Ellen's presence was once again welcome. "Sure, yes, obviously." Cynthia touched the back of the girl's tiny, exposed neck, turning a nervous eye to the clock and just imagining Matt's face if he walked in here to see Cynthia had brought the child to tears again.

"We can be that good kind of family. The kind you get to pick for yourself. Please, Abby, don't be upset. You were right." Jennifer was going to *love* this.

Abby didn't look up but ran a hand under her nose. Then across the tablecloth, Cynthia couldn't help noticing.

"Is it the kind of family that gets their picture up on the wall?" The voice was teeny.

"What?"

"I want my picture up on the wall like everyone else's." Abby pointed to the explosion of framed photos that covered one whole side of Cynthia's living room, the newest one of Matt, grimacing in a cap and gown, taking momentary centre stage.

"I want to be that kind of family."

Cynthia let out the air she had been unknowingly holding since the conversation began and smiled as she saw Ellen lean over her chair and riffle through her purse, pulling out a digital camera. She was a mean old broad when she wanted to be, but that woman had a heart of gold.

Cynthia grabbed Abby's hand, taking her over to the sink to clean up her face that began to beam at the sight of the camera. How delightfully simple and straightforward the world looks to a ten-year-old; how devastatingly lonely and sad. Yet this was a time in life when wrongs could so easily be set to right. She led the girl into the living room and sat with her on the couch, Ellen following behind and setting the camera on the mantelpiece before joining them.

"We are definitely that kind of family."

Acknowledgements

MUCH GRATITUDE TO MY FAMILY AND FRIENDS FOR THEIR constant support and cheerleading. A special thanks to Allister Thompson, Sylvia McConnell, Emma Dolan, and the Dundurn team. Thanks to the members of the 296 Supper Club and the Browning Crew for the inspiration, the laughs, and the great meals.

The Year She Left
by Kerry Kelly
978-1894917728
$19.95

Is it a happy ending? Define happy. Stuart Lewis, thirty-three, in love, and content, wakes up one day to find his fiancée has left him. Perpetually underemployed and now homeless, Stuart moves onto his mother's couch. With few connections and no ambition, Stuart is forced to rethink the choices he has made and the sincerity of the life that has just been shattered. Set against the frigid backdrop of downtown Toronto, *The Year She Left* casts an eclectic bunch of directionless underachievers and unlikely heroes amid the buzz of late-night binges and early corporate bustle. Honest and unapologetic about the often detached nature of youthful urban existence, this is the story of what happened in the year she left.

The Space Between
by j.p. Rodriguez
978-1894917889
$19.95

Two wrongs may not make a right, but what about three?
Rodriguez's debut is an examination of what it means to
live a modern life and the price of inaction in a world where
chances at redemption and happiness are all too few. The
narrator came early to understand that every action creates
a reaction, and what goes up comes down — usually hard.
So he's spent his life in an emotional straitjacket, living
comfortably on the surface. Only once has he ever come
close to betraying his philosophy, but he came to his senses
before it was too late and left her. At least that's what
he thinks until the morning he wakens to a violent and
inexplicable nausea. Haunted by the love he threw away
and his former lover's mysterious murder, he leaves his job
and sets off in search of direction. On an epic journey over
land and sea, through past and present, his heart and mind
struggle to find common ground. Mile by mile, he develops
the justification for an act of deliberate violence and maybe
his own redemption.

Reinventing the Rose
by Kenneth J. Harvey
978-1554889211
$22.99

As a fatherless girl with a mother who persistently encouraged her daughter's artistic temperament, Anna Wells is highly sensitive to the life developing in her when she discovers she is pregnant. Anna's gynecologist boyfriend, Kevin, considers the time just not right to have children, so Anna moves to a 100-year-old house in Bareneed, an abandoned cove in Newfoundland, where she takes comfort in renovating the interior of her new home and working on a series of paintings detailing roses.

Paralleling Anna's own journey is a minutely detailed, day-by-day development of the embryo. All goes well until a car arrives delivering a court summons. Kevin has filed a statement of claim seeking the termination of the embryo as "return of property." One night, while still in Bareneed and upset over the impending legal action, Anna discovers an abandoned little girl almost frozen to death in her front yard. Mysterious circumstances continue to surround the children in Bareneed as pro-choice and pro-life factions marshal their forces.

DUNDURN
www.dundurn.com

What did you think of this book?
Visit www.dundurn.com for
reviews, videos, updates, and more!